DEATH ON THE DOORSTEP

DEATH ON
THE DOORSTEP

by

George Douglas

Dales Large Print Books
Long Preston, North Yorkshire,
BD23 4ND, England.

British Library Cataloguing in Publication Data.

Douglas, George
    Death on the doorstep.

    A catalogue record of this book is
    available from the British Library

    ISBN   1-84262-342-7 pbk

First published in Great Britain in 1973
by Robert Hale & Company

Copyright © George Douglas 1973

Cover illustration © Andy Walker by arrangement with
P.W.A. International Ltd.

The moral right of the author has been asserted

Published in Large Print 2004 by arrangement with
Robert Hale Ltd.

Dales Large Print is an imprint of Library Magna Books Ltd.

Printed and bound in Great Britain by
T.J. (International) Ltd., Cornwall, PL28 8RW

Chapter One

At seven o'clock the alarm shrilled and William Holder, retired schoolmaster, woke on its first beat, swung himself out of bed and silenced the clock in one movement. He turned to tuck the disturbed bedclothes round his still-sleeping wife, put on slippers and dressing gown, paid a brief visit to the bathroom and padded alertly downstairs, a small, slim man with thick white hair, a large nose and a firm chin. There was just enough light on this mid-November morning for him to reach the kitchen without groping.

There, he switched on the ceiling lamp, filled the electric kettle and set it going, then, as was his custom, he unbolted the back door to take a look at the morning. The air was crisply cool, the trees at the end of the garden were just visible. He glanced casually downwards and stiffened, his heart beginning to race. The body of a man lay sprawled half in and half out of the back porch. Holder took a deep breath to steady himself, bent down and touched one of the outflung hands. The fingers were cold and stiff. He said, explosively, 'Flaming hell!' and hurried to the foot of the stairs where the telephone sat on a window ledge.

Detective Inspector Mallin of the Benfield City Police was also awakened that morning by a bell. Surfacing to consciousness, he killed the sound by lifting the receiver of the telephone on his bedside table. He grunted an acknowledgement, listened, said, 'Inform Sergeant Lee. Tell him I'll meet him there.' He switched on the light and heaved himself out of bed like a buffalo leaving its wallow.

Even in crumpled pyjamas and with short-cut greying hair a tousled mess he looked a policeman. He was big, beefy, hard-featured, fit as a butcher's dog. He leaned over the twin bed where his tiny, slightly-built wife was still sleeping, and shook her vigorously.

'Wake up, Linda! A bloke's got himself shot, Northfield way.'

Linda Mallin turned on her back, blinking her eyes against the light.

'How dreadful, dear. Anybody we know?' And then, as the significance of her husband's words penetrated, she shot up from the bedclothes.

'You don't mean–? But it's your rest day. They can't do this to us! We were going to

8

have a trip up the Dales to see the autumn colours, remember?'

'That'll have to wait,' Mallin was already on his way to the bathroom. 'I'll make do with a pot of tea and some toast this morning – in a hurry, please!'

Linda Mallin sighed, and reached for her housecoat. Twenty-five minutes later her husband's cream Renault was backing down the drive of their neat semi in Greystone Crescent.

Mallin knew the Northfield district well, he had served a spell at the sub-station there. He remembered Dainford Road, one of the small nucleus of houses which had been put up just before the war. Then, they were surrounded by fields and woodlands – an extremely select area. But the city had bulged outwards, and now Northfield was just one more featureless suburb, a small and ugly dormitory town itself, with only the Dainford Road area to speak of its former glories.

That road, now a link between two thoroughfares, was streaming with business-going cars when Mallin turned into it at half past eight. The drivers of those cars spared a quick look of curiosity at the two police vehicles drawn up outside Number 20.

There was another car occupying the drive, and as he swung in behind it, Mallin recognized the dark blue Viva de Luxe which belonged to his assistant, Detective Sergeant Lee. Mallin got out of his car, walked round to the back of the house. On a concreted area which separated the house from the garden four men were standing, watching a fifth manoeuvring a camera trained on a crumpled heap of clothes and outspread limbs which took up most of the small back porch. A chorus of 'Good morning sir!' greeted the inspector and a tall, fair, blue-eyed man came forward. Brian Lee, whose nickname in the Force was 'Bonny,' looked his super-handsome self even at this hour of the day. He made his report briskly and without preamble, because he knew that was the way Mallin wanted it.

'The occupant, Mr William Holder, found the body there just after seven, sir. Bailey and Forbes' – a thumb indicated the two uniformed men in the group – 'were directed here to take over. Dr Lazenby has already been and gone, he lives only a few streets away. Cause of death, bullet in brain, the man was shot between the eyes. Time of death, between eight and twelve last night. Provisional, of course, as usual. Coates has done his sketches, and Scott has just about finished. Ambulance on its way.'

'Identified?'

'Not yet, sir. He's not known to any of us here, nor to Mr Holder.'

'Right.' Mallin turned to the photographer. 'Scott?'

'I've got all I can, sir. It's a bit difficult, the way he's lying in this porch.'

'You and Coates can push off, then. Bailey, ring in and say I'm keeping you and Forbes here for the present. But before you do, let's have him out on this concrete.'

The patrolmen lifted the body out of the porch, laid it down as Mallin indicated. The inspector nodded to Lee.

'See what he's got on him.'

The haul was meagre and not particularly helpful. A worn wallet held four pound notes, a small fold-up calendar of the current year, a card, issued by a brewers' company, of the fixtures of Benfield United Football Club, a buff-coloured receipt from one of the city's multiple stores and a grimy piece of paper with '6 crysants 2 doz daylys' scrawled on it in pencil. In the pockets were also a crumpled handkerchief, a large treble-bladed pocketknife, some loose change, a small hank of green string and a

11

key ring with three keys on it.

Mallin picked up the receipt, unfolded it and read it aloud. 'Office Copy, Wellards Limited, dated last April. One Panther, seven pounds ninety-five. Paid.' He cocked an eyebrow at young Forbes. 'Seems clear what his job was, doesn't it?'

Forbes hesitated. He was in a dilemma. He knew the correct answer, which wasn't the one Mallin was expecting him to give. Should he, therefore, lay himself open to a correction from the inspector, which it would afford Mallin intense satisfaction to give, or should he show that he wasn't such a mug, after all? To hell with tactfulness. He plunged.

'Not a dealer in wild animals, sir, despite that receipt. My father owns a Panther – a lawn mower. The green string, the knife and the paper with the flower names on it suggests a gardener to me, sir.'

'Fair enough.' Mallin didn't seem at all disappointed that he hadn't caught the young man out. 'How about the keys?'

'One Yale latch key and two car keys, sir.'

'And that,' Mallin said, 'is about all this lot tells us. That he wasn't a vagrant – clothes and shoes, I mean, and the money in his wallet. That he bought a lawn mower last

12

spring and that his handwriting is vile and his spelling atrocious. Yep?' Bailey had come round the corner of the house.

'Ambulance here, sir.'

'Right. We'd better shift our cars, Lee, so's the driver can back right up to here. You take charge of the bloke's possessions.'

Manoeuvring was carried out and the ambulance crew did their work quickly, efficiently. As they moved away, Mallin said to Lee, 'You've seen this chap Holder, who found the body?'

'Briefly, sir. I thought I'd wait until you arrived and we'd done all the preliminaries. He seems a sensible chap, he said he and his wife would keep out of the way until we were ready to talk to them.'

Mallin nodded, told the patrolmen to stand by and walked with his sergeant to the back door. His knock was answered by the white-haired Holder. From behind his floated a mouth-watering smell of eggs and bacon.

'Come in, gentlemen.' Holder composed his once-handsome face into serious lines as he stepped back to give them entry into a warm, shining kitchen with a small table set up in the middle of it which bore the remains of breakfast. A fresh-complexioned woman of Holder's age, with shining brown hair shot with white, rose from the table and smiled a welcome.

'My wife,' Holder said, and Lee introduced his inspector.

'Sorry to interrupt your meal.' Mallin's apology was briskly formal. 'But we have to talk to you, of course.'

'We've just finished,' Mrs Holder returned. 'Take them into the sittingroom, Bill. Two large men make this place look very much overcrowded.'

They followed Holder into a large room, the furniture of which spoke of the middle nineteen-twenties, with the addition of a storage heater and a colour television set. Holder waved them to comfortable chairs and switched on an electric fire in the hearth. He sat down in a smaller chair, facing them.

'Now, sir,' Mallin began, 'I know you've spoken to Sergeant Lee, but I'd like to hear the story again from you.'

Holder nodded. 'There's not much to tell. I came downstairs at seven, opened the back door and there he was. I telephoned you people at once, roused my wife, went and had another look at him, without touching nor disturbing anything. Then the two policemen arrived and they took over.'

'You had another look at him,' Mallin repeated. 'Finding a dead body on your doorstep didn't shock or upset you, then?'

'It wasn't the most pleasant way to begin the day, I must admit. But I was naturally curious. And during the last war I was in Civil Defence, and as you know, Benfield took quite a few hammerings. I got used to dealing with dead bodies then.'

'But you didn't recognize this one, obviously, or you'd have told us so before now?'

Holder paused before he answered. 'He was shot, wasn't he? Neatly, between the eyes. The face wasn't damaged... No, I didn't recognize him as far as being able to give him a name, but I'm certain I've seen him before.'

'In this district, sir?'

'Maybe so. Wouldn't swear to it, though. Anyway, you'll probably know who he is by now. I mean, you'll have searched him?'

'He carried no personal identification on him at all, sir. However, we've taken photographs and when they're developed we'll ask you to look at some of them. They may jog your memory. Now, it seems certain he was shot before midnight last night. That could have been done at your back door, or he may have been killed elsewhere and

15

dumped on you. You heard no unusual sounds?'

'None whatsoever. Nor did my wife, we've already discussed the point. As usual, we spent the evening in this room, reading and watching television. I make it a rule, when the evenings become dark early, to lock and bolt the back door, and put the chain up, before we settle down in here. That is normally before six o'clock. We go to bed between ten and half past.'

Lee sat forward in his chair. 'This isn't exactly a secluded road, sir. I take it there is traffic up and down it until quite late in the evening?'

'It's very well used, Sergeant. Rather different from when we first came to live here, nearly forty years ago!' He smiled wryly.

'So, to carry a body along your drive and round to the back door would mean a risk of being seen from the road, or from the windows of your neighbours' houses opposite. Is there a back way into your garden?'

'None at all. The gardens here join on to those in Dainford Close. There is a high panelled fence between them and us. We are also fenced off from our neighbours at either side.'

Mallin swung his bulk on to his feet. 'So

that seems as far as we can go at the moment, Mr Holder. We'll have a look at those fences before we leave, and we'll be in touch with you again. You're retired, I take it?'

'Yes. I was a schoolmaster, for my sins. But when my sixtieth birthday came up, nine years ago, I packed it in with promptitude and great joy.'

'Thanks for being so helpful.' They went out through the kitchen and Mallin paused for a word with Mrs Holder, now busy with washing up. A quick tour round an immaculately-kept garden showed no signs of disturbance. Mallin led the way back to the front of the house, pausing on the drive.

'Why here, Bonny?' The question, Lee knew, was rhetorical. He said, 'Of the two alternatives, sir, I'm inclined to go for the one which says he was shot at the back door, not killed first and dumped there.'

'Me, too... Something about the way the body was lying... Which means that our Panther-buying friend was paying a visit to this house. He chose the back door rather than the front. Was he on a quick doing-over of the kitchen and dining-room while the Holders were engrossed in their telly?'

'I suppose that's possible. No break-in tools, though, if you except his big knife.'

17

'He went to the back door and there he was shot dead. So somebody was following him or waiting for him. This could be a tough one, Bonny.' He sighed, and moved on. 'The usual house-to-house, I suppose, but we'll get a supply of those photographs first. So it's back to HQ to report and set up the organization.'

He sent the patrolmen on their way before he got into his car. 'No need for you to hang about,' he told them, and, with Lee's car following, he made the best speed he could through the Wednesday morning traffic to their headquarters at Benfield Central, where Detective Superintendent Trott, lean and with a sunken-cheeked face which underlined a naturally gloomy disposition, received them in his office.

'I found the initial message on my pad.' He glared at his visitors as if this were their fault. 'I've also had a report from Scott and Coates when they came in. Any developments?'

'No, sir,' Mallin answered. 'We think he was shot where he was found. No identification. No personal papers on him.'

Trott sighed deeply. 'As if we hadn't enough work on our plates as it is.' He glanced at a handwritten list on his desk. 'I can let you have Danby and Jones. And

18

WDC Radley, if you think she'd be of any use. And you, Lee, of course.' He turned to Mallin. 'What about it, Tom? It's your rest day, I know.'

'That's mucked up already. I'll get it in later. If we can make a quick break on this job—'

He was interrupted by a knock on the door and the entrance of Scott, the photographer. He put a small pile of pictures on the desk.

'Half a dozen for showing around, sir. The rest are routine positions, all in duplicate. We've touched up the first lot to make him look alive.'

The 'first lot' showed a youngish man – Lee guessed his age as around thirty – with fair short hair which was already receding above a narrow forehead. The nose was long and slightly crooked, the mouth wide, loose-lipped. 'We haven't his dabs on the local file, by the way,' Scott added.

'Nice job,' Trott's gloom lightened momentarily. 'So you can get your gang together, Lee.'

'Yes, sir.' Lee picked up four of the photographs and left the room. DC's Jones and Danby were in the general office, busy with paperwork. 'Where's that girl Sylvia?' Lee asked.

19

'Er – just slipped down to the canteen, Sarge,' Danby answered. 'I mean, it's coffee-break time, isn't it?'

'Not today. We've a rush job on. You go and haul her back here. And hurry!'

Danby, a round-faced, fresh-complexioned young man, grinned and disappeared promptly. Jones began to pack his work away without comment. He was a heavily-built man in his middle thirties, stolid, sparing of speech, but eminently dependable.

Mallin came into the office on the heels of the returning Danby who was accompanied by Woman Detective Constable Radley, brown-haired, grey-eyed and new to the CID. Mallin, who knew his sergeant would have given neither information nor instruction until all his forces were assembled, took over.

He outlined the facts briefly. 'It'll be the usual house-to-house "Do you know this man?" routine.' He swung round to Jones. 'Map!'

For all his bulk, Jones could move swiftly, effortlessly. A couple of strides took him to the indexed map-rack, he unclipped one of its sheets and brought it to the empty desk to which Mallin had stepped. The map, a sixteen inches to the mile OS issue, was laid on the desk. The others gathered round it.

'Here's Dainford Road.' Mallin's forefinger descended accurately. 'Number 20 here. You'll take the Road itself first, Sergeant, with Miss Radley. Danby and Jones this parallel one, Dainford Way. Then, if necessary, Dainford Close – here – and Moorland Lane – here. After that, we'll see. I'm coming with you. My car, which will be your base, will be parked at this end of Dainford Road. Let's get moving.'

Lee packed Danby, Jones and Sylvia Radley into the Viva, after a glance at the official car park which showed, at that time of day, a dearth of vehicles. The Viva was new, he was secretly very proud of it and not at all averse to exhibiting its paces. But Mallin, with a couple of minutes' start, was at the top of Dainford Road before them. Lee drew up behind him and his passengers spilled out. He handed photographs round.

'I'll take the even numbers side here,' he told Sylvia. 'You the odds. You know the routine?'

The girl smiled at him. Women found it easy to smile at Bonny Lee.

'Sure, Sarge. Flash warrant card, apologize for troubling them, show photograph – do you know, etc. If no dice, evade curious

21

enquiries by muttering vaguely about a missing person who may be in the district, thank 'em, get away smartly.'

'Just like that. And I'll bet I'll beat you to the end of the street.' He turned away to tackle the first house.

There were twelve houses on each side of Dainford Road, a mixture of semis and detached villas. Lee missed out the Holders' place, but as he came away from Number 24 he found Sylvia waiting for him.

'I should have taken that bet, Sarge. Though I've got to admit to no reply from three houses. At number 7 the woman hesitated a bit and said she'd an idea she'd seen the man somewhere, then she took that back and said on second thoughts she hadn't. All the rest were blanks.'

'I didn't even get a maybe.' Lee shrugged ruefully. 'So we walk back up the road and spill our news to Mr Mallin. Like another bet? That he won't jump for joy when he hears it?'

Mallin put down the newspaper he had been reading and stuck his head out of the car window.

'Right,' he said before Lee could speak. 'So it's Dainford Crescent for you next. We'll give it another hour before we knock off for some refreshment. There's quite a good pub– Hang on a minute, though.'

Jones and Danby were hurrying towards them and Danby's round face was beaming sunnily. But, when they reached the car it was the stolid Jones who reported.

'Positive identification, sir. Woman named Norton, 35 Dainford Way. Dead man's name is Wilfred Dawson, worked there as a gardener three days a week. I told her he'd been in an accident – nothing else. Checked neighbours on each side, also identified him as the Nortons' gardener.'

'Good. Sergeant Lee and I will go along there. You three can get back to HQ. There's a bus stop over yonder, quarter hour service. If you hurry you'll just catch the next one to town.'

Chapter Two

The house in Dainford Way was detached, with a lawn in front and borders which ran back from the road at each side of it. Lee's ring at the bell brought a tall, gaunt woman to the door. She had a grim, severe look about her and she wore a black dress, heavy shoes and a plastic apron.

Lee put on his smile. 'Good morning. Mrs Norton?'

'My name's Carr. I work here, weekday mornings. You more police? We've had a man here already. About Dawson.'

'And now you've got two more.' When he cared to use it, Mallin had an intimidating growl. 'So you tell Mrs Norton we want to talk to her, eh?'

She sniffed. The growl had misfired for once. 'Better come in, I suppose. She's upstairs. I'll get her down here.' She opened a sliding glass door which led into a sitting-room from the white-painted, grey-carpeted hall. A jerk of her head invited them to enter, and she closed the door behind them.

'Bit of money here.' Mallin ranged round the large room, glancing at a display of Coalport china in a cabinet, at a mantelpiece crowded with Georgian silver, at the modern furniture and fittings. Flowers, mostly chrysanthemums and late-blooming roses, were everywhere, in cut-glass vases in side tables, on the wide bow-fronted window-ledge, in brass containers which filled the corners. Then a door opened from an inner room and a plump woman in her early fifties came in. The auburn of her immaculately-set hair had obviously come from a bottle, her smudgy grey eyes were pearl shaded. She wore blunt-toed wedge shoes and her russet dress had very certainly not been bought at a department store. Mallin stepped forward to introduce himself and Lee.

'Do please sit down.' She waved a heavily-beringed hand at them and her voice came out in a rush of highly-pitched words. Mallin hitched up his trousers and sub-sided in an armchair while Lee brought forward a smaller one. Mrs Norton sank on to a large leather pouffe at one side of the fireplace, where a gas fire added to the already powerful central heating. 'I've already heard the dreadful news, of course. About Wilfred, I mean. Is he seriously? In hospital? I really

25

must go to see him.'

'Wilfred Dawson is worse than hurt, madam.' Mallin paused to give her a chance to take that in. Then he added, 'I'm sorry to have to tell you he's dead. It's a case of homicide, and–'

Mrs Norton interrupted him by falling sideways off her pouffe in a faint.

It was characteristic of Mallin that, while Lee sprang up and went to her assistance, he sat without moving, only raising his voice in a full-throated bellow of 'Mrs Carr!' The 'daily' appeared so quickly as to give cause for suspicion that she had been listening outside the door which led into the kitchen. Between them, she and Lee got the lady of the house into a chair where she moaned, fluttered her eyelids and was able to swallow, with speed, the glass of brandy Mrs Carr provided. There was an interval of cosseting, murmurs of apology from Mrs Norton and a half-hearted suggestion from Mallin that they should come back later, when Mrs Norton would feel fit enough to talk to them. Mrs Norton waved her hands at him.

'Certainly not, Inspector… Just a moment of weakness… The shock, you know. I'm quite all right now.' She smiled bravely. 'I'm

26

sure, if Mrs Carr would be good enough to make us all some coffee...'

Mrs Carr said, 'Couple of minutes,' and disappeared, taking the brandy with her.

'Dreadful of me,' Mrs Norton went on. 'Of course, I'm at the age... And Wilfred was such a nice boy, he's been a real pillar of strength to us. This large garden, you know, he kept it immaculate. I don't know how we shall ever replace him.' She sat forward. 'But do tell me what happened. I promise faithfully I won't misbehave again.'

By the time coffee had been brought in, handed round and sipped, Mrs Norton had the main facts of Dawson's death given to her by Lee, while the policemen had learnt, from questions by Mallin, that Mrs Norton was childless, that her husband was managing director of the Benfield Wire Rope and Cable Company in Saville Street and that they had lived in Dainford Way for the past twenty-five years.

'My husband was attracted by the garden, it was his only hobby. Then, two years ago, he had a fall at work and damaged his spine. The doctors forbade him to do any more digging or unnecessary physical work. We advertised in the Benfield Chronicle for a part-time gardener and Wilfred – poor lad, I can't believe it yet – turned up.'

'There was nothing on him to indicate his address,' Mallin said. 'You'll be able to supply us with that?'

Her forehead creased in a frown. 'I'm afraid not. He lived somewhere just outside Benfield, but he never said just where. But he did tell me his father had a large farm, though he himself preferred gardening to farming, so had set up his own little business. He had a small van, you see. A green one. An Austin 35, I think.'

'He worked here three days a week. Winter as well as summer?'

'Er – yes. We have a large heated greenhouse and he was always able to find winter work about the place. Tree pruning, and so on, and he did odd jobs about the house.'

'He'd mention his other employers to you, people for whom he worked for the rest of the week, of course?'

'I think he spoke of some people named Atkinson, but I've a shocking memory for names. Anyway, it was at some large estate in the Westhill district. He ran the whole of it, single-handed.'

'Quite a worker,' Mallin said drily. 'So you'd say he was in the self-employed class?'

'Oh, yes. I mean, I paid him, but there

wasn't any question of providing insurance stamps.'

'I see. You'll be good enough, I'm sure, to allow Sergeant Lee to use your telephone?' Mrs Norton said, 'Of course,' and showed her surprise when Lee got up and went into the hall without a word. Mallin grinned crookedly.

'We've worked together for quite a while now, ma'am. We can just about read each other's thoughts. Not a bad-looking chap, Sergeant Lee, eh?'

The beringed hands came together. 'I think he's absolutely gorgeous!' She tittered, then composed her face into solemn lines and sighed. 'Wilfred always worked stripped to the waist in summer. He had a beautiful body. I shall miss him, he was such a good friend. He would do anything for me.'

'You talked to him a lot?'

'Yes. I – we – looked on him almost as one of the family. You see, Mrs Carr only comes in the mornings and I don't go out much. I suffer a great deal from my nerves, Inspector. I get tense, strung up. Wilfred could always relax me, just by talking to me, giving me his company, if you see what I mean.'

'Which days of the week did he work here?'

'Mondays, Wednesdays and Fridays. He never missed.'

'So he wouldn't meet your husband often, I suppose?'

'No. Julian – Mr Norton – would tell me what he wanted done in the garden and I'd tell Wilf. But sometimes, if my husband decided he'd like a big job done – some alteration or re-designing – Wilf would come here on a Sunday morning and they would talk it over together.'

'Mr Dawson would tell you about his friends, his hobbies, and so on? Was he married?'

'Oh, no. He used to say, "I'm a born bachelor, Mrs Norton."' She smiled sadly. 'He didn't talk about his family much, though there is a brother who is a judge in Canada. Wilf liked to go dancing occasionally, or have a night out with the boys, as he used to say.' Tears glittered behind her eyelids. 'He was such a nice boy, Inspector!'

Mallin had heard Lee finish his call, had been conscious for some minutes of his sergeant's voice in the kitchen. But now Lee came through the door from the hall, caught Mallin's eye and nodded. Mallin stood up.

'We won't take up any more of your time, ma'am. You've been helpful. There's no doubt in your mind, by the way, that the photograph you were shown is that of Wilfred Dawson?'

'Good heavens, no, Inspector! Mrs Carr recognized him at once, too. Besides, it's Wednesday and he hasn't turned up here today. He's always made a point of ringing me if something has prevented him from coming on one of his days. I was only just saying to Mrs Carr, when the man called with the photograph, that Wilfred was late arriving. And…'

The tears flowed over now and Mallin and Lee made as rapid an exit as decency allowed. But they walked very slowly down the drive to the inspector's car in which they had both travelled from town.

'Well?' Mallin asked.

'The Ministry of Social Security people were very helpful, sir. They haven't a Wilfred Dawson registered as a self-employed gardener, but they dug out a man of that name as a scrap-metal merchant. That could possibly fit, all the other self-employed Dawsons in their files seem to be right out. The address is Hawes Street. I had a word with Mrs Carr in the kitchen. She obviously had no use for Dawson. Said he was the biggest liar in creation and couldn't

31

do an honest day's work to save his life. But he'd wormed his way in here and was the real blue-eyed boy as far as Mrs Norton was concerned.'

'Any suggestions that Mrs Norton and he were playing games?'

'I did drop a hint to that effect but Mrs Carr didn't pick it up. She clammed up after she'd got what I've told you off her chest.'

'Mrs Norton took a real wallop when she heard he was dead,' Mallin said thoughtfully. 'Might be an idea to have a quiet word with the neighbours on each side of the house.' He stood by the car, swinging his key ring on one finger. Then he shrugged. 'We'll leave it for now. Let's pay another call on Holder while we're in the district. He seemed to think Dawson's face was familiar. You've got one of those touched-up shots with you?'

Lee nodded, and got into the car.

They found Holder, the retired school-master, cutting off the dead perennial stems in his front garden. He came to the gate to meet them, his face one large question.

'We've got an identification of the man who was shot,' Mallin told him. 'Name of Wilfred Dawson. You said–'

'Dawson! Of course!' Holder smacked a fist into his other palm and nodded vigorously as he peered at the photograph Lee was holding out to him. 'He was in my class at Farley Street School for two years. That would be – let's see – about sixteen or seventeen years ago. One tends to remember the bad lads rather than the good ones, you know.'

'Bit of a villain, was he?'

'I wouldn't say that, Inspector. I mean, he was normally well-behaved in class. But he was the biggest liar I think I ever came across. You just couldn't believe a word he said. A sly, oily customer with it, too. But de mortuis and all that, I suppose.'

'Not in this case, sir. We've got to find out all we can about him. Do you happen to know what job he did when he left school?'

'I can't call that to mind. He was what I always classified as the errand boy type. But I saw him, some two years later, behind a secondhand stall in the Markets. We had a few minutes' chat and he told me he was about to go into the scrap-metal trade in a big way. I didn't believe him, of course.'

'It could be just possible he was speaking the truth then, sir. But that's for us to find out. What about his background – as a schoolboy, I mean?'

'Fairly average for the Farley Street district in those days. Father in and out of work, mother a bit of a slattern, judging by the boy's clothes and general appearance. Young Dawson always struck me as a possible future petty crook type, bit of a wide boy, as the phrase had it then.' He tapped the photograph. 'Oh, that's the Dawson I taught, all right.'

'And he was found dead at your back door,' Lee commented. 'You told us, sir, that you've lived here for a long time, forty years, wasn't it?'

Holder nodded. 'Hard to realize, but it's true.'

'Would it be possible that Dawson knew you lived here?'

Holder did his fist-smacking act again. 'More than possible, I'd say. You see, about fifteen years ago, when I had Dawson in my class, this district hadn't been developed. Countryside all around us then. I've always been a keen walker and I like to see children use their legs. I used to organize hikes from school on summer Saturdays. Twice, while Dawson was my pupil, I brought the class up here for a cross-country walk, and we finished at this house where my wife provided tea for the gang. Dawson came on both occasions.'

'What Sergeant Lee has in mind,' Mallin

said, 'is that, knowing where you lived, Dawson came here last night to see you. Would he do such a thing if, say he was in trouble and thought you'd help him?'

Holder considered. 'That's quite an angle, isn't it? Yes, from what I know of him he might have done so.' He cleared his throat. 'I – er – Well, that Farley Street district wasn't one of ideal home life, I'm afraid. D'you know, a lot of my lads hardly ever spoke to their parents – to confide in them, or ask advice? Their elders just couldn't be bothered with them. So when the youngsters had problems they brought them to me. I encouraged this and I think – I hope – that in some cases I was helpful.'

'No doubt of that, I'm sure,' Mallin said heartily. He glanced at his watch. 'We'll be getting along, Mr Holder. Thanks for what you've told us.'

In the car, headed back for town, Mallin said, 'It's a possible reason why Dawson was found on that doorstep. Though you'd think he'd have gone to the front door. Or, better still, to his friend Mrs Norton, if he was in serious trouble.'

'Maybe he didn't want her to know about it, sir. It could have spoilt her image of him.'

Mallin grunted. 'We'll go and check that

address the Ministry people gave you. Hawes Street. Number Four district, isn't it? We'll use the Southway Ring Road – quicker than crawling through the middle of town.'

Hawes Street was part of a council house estate which had grown up as a result of the city's earliest attempt at slum clearance and rehousing in the middle thirties. It was worn and somewhat tatty now, the brickwork of its houses blackened and chipped, its small front gardens, in the main, neglected. But here and there pride still reigned, in a clipped hedge, a mown lawn, brightly coloured window curtains. Number 3 claimed this rating and Mallin nodded with satisfaction at the scratched and battered green A 35 van which stood outside the small gate.

'Dawson's vehicle, odds on.' He drew up behind it.

Lee's knock brought a girl in her teens to the door. Lank pale hair hung at each side of her plain face. Drowned eyes and a red-tipped nose showed she was, in the local phrase, lost in a cold. She sniffed and regarded them with no apparent interest.

Lee put on a smile for her. 'Good morning. Does Mr Wilfred Dawson live here?'

'Aye.' She blew into a crumpled hand-

36

kerchief. 'But he i'n't at home. Went off out last night and didn't come back. So what?'

Mallin stepped forward. 'We're police officers. We'd like a word with you. May we come in?'

'S'pose so.' She turned her head and yelled, 'Mum! Coupla coppers here. Better come and see what they want, hadn't yer?'

She stepped aside to let them into a narrow passageway, lino-covered, with a flight of stairs at one end and a door flanking them. A stout, brassy-haired woman came through the door, wiping her hands on a towel. She looked at the two men for a moment, her head cocked on one side, then she threw the towel to the girl, said, 'You go into the kitchen, Greta.' The girl pushed past her and the woman opened a door on her left.

'We'll go in here,' she said, with a token glance at the warrant card Lee pushed under her nose. 'It's about Wilf, eh?'

She preceded them into what was clearly the main living room of the house, large, square, with a worn carpet, a three piece suite which looked new, a television set and an oval, imitation-mahogany table. She turned up the gas fire in the hearth and waved the CID men to the armchairs of the suite. Then she sat primly down on the settee between them.

Mallin said his official introduction piece. 'And you, madam are–?'

'Mrs Saunders. Mary Saunders. That was my daughter Greta as let you in. I'm a widow, lost my husband three years ago. Lung cancer. Like I said, you've come about Wilf, haven't you?'

Mallin nodded solemnly, and Lee produced his photograph.

'Mr Wilfred Dawson,' Mallin continued. 'That him?'

'It is.' She handed the print back and smoothed her dress over her knees. 'Our lodger. And you can tell me the worst, mister. I know it's got to be bad or you wouldn't be here showing photos of him. Go on, I can take it.'

'He's dead, Mrs Saunders. He was killed last night.'

The blood left her florid face and her hands clenched on her knees. They gave her time to recover herself, which, Lee thought, wouldn't take long. She'd had hard knocks before, he guessed, maybe plenty of them. She sighed relaxed a little, began to regain her colour.

'Traffic accident? We've bin wondering, seeing he didn't come home last night.'

38

'Worse than that. He was found shot, up Northfield way.'

'You mean at that place where he worked, gardening? I've warned him that one day her husband 'ud find out and...' She clamped her lips tightly together.

'You've got it wrong,' Mallin told her. 'However, we'll come to that later. And, since I seem to have been talking all morning, I'll let Sergeant Lee ask the questions.' He sat back in his chair but kept his eyes on Mrs Saunders' face.

'Dawson lodged here,' Lee began. 'For how long?'

'Must be well over two years now. When my husband died, I got the Council's permission to take a lodger. I put an advert in our paper shop and Wilf saw it and come here.'

'Where had he been living until then?' Lee wasn't taking notes. He had the power of perfect recall for conversational details.

'With his parents, in Sheffield. He said his dad owned a steel factory there. Wanted Will to go into the business. Wilf tried it for a few years, then chucked it up. Fancied more of an outdoor life, he said.'

'Do you know his home address, Mrs Saunders?'

She shook her glinting head. 'I don't. I asked him once why he never wrote home, nor got any letters and he said his folks, like himself, were poor letter writers but that he always rang them twice a week, keeping in touch, like.'

'What did he work at when he wasn't gardening out Northfield?'

'He ran some sort of scrap metal business. Him and a partner. But he never said much about it so I can't tell you who the partner was or where they ran the business from. But I reckon they weren't doing very well, which is why he took up this gardening job about two years ago.'

'Tell us what sort of a fellow he was.'

'Quiet about the house, clean habits, easy to get on with. Bragged a bit sometimes, he did, and I can't say I believed all he told me. But we got along all right. I'll be lucky if I get another lodger as good.'

'How did he spent his spare time?'

'Went out three, four evenings a week. Fond of dancing, he was. He used to go to that spot in Carlton Street a lot, High Swing or something, they call it. According to him, he was very pally with the chap that runs it.'

'And the other evenings, Mrs Saunders?'

'Oh, he might stay in and watch the telly

with me and Greta, or he'd say he'd some business to do and go off in his van. Weekends – well, it was a case of the scrap metal job on Saturdays, and Sundays he'd have a lie in till dinnertime and then sort of hang around for the rest of the day.'

'Did he bring friends to the house?'

She shook her head. 'Never.'

'What about girls?'

'He didn't seem interested in them. I thought, once over, him and our Greta... But it didn't come to nothing. Wilf reckoned he preferred what he called mature women. That's why I thought, when you said the poor lad had been shot... But that's none of my business.'

'It's ours, though,' Mallin broke in sharply. 'This is a case of homicide, Mrs Saunders. So you'll tell us all you know.'

Chapter Three

She looked from Mallin to Lee and nodded. 'That's fair enough, I s'pose. You want to get whoever killed him and I want to see you do just that.' She smoothed her dress down again.

'Well, this scrap metal job wasn't going too brilliantly, and he sees this advert for a part-time gardener and gets started on there. Very soon he was telling us what a snip it was. The place wasn't all that big and he could do more or less what he liked with it. He hardly ever saw the man of the family, the missus used to pay him. She had money of her own, Wilf said, and would always slip him a few quid extra every week, over and above what he'd agreed to work for.

'But not only that. He'd work in the mornings, while her daily woman was there, but he'd spend most afternoons in the house talking to this woman. "Just talking?" our Greta said to him once, cheeky-like, and he said, "Them as don't know can't tell," and winked at her. Oh, and he used to buy plants and that for the garden and she paid him and never asked to see the bills. He reckoned to make anything up to twenty quid a week there. Got his dinner there, too. He paid me ten, so what with the scrap metal business as well, he was doing all right.'

'You think he was having an affair with his employer, Mrs Saunders?'

'I couldn't rightly tell you, Sergeant. To hear him talk, well, she'd do anything he wanted, but then again, you couldn't always believe what he said.'

'Did he ever mention a Mr Holder, a former schoolmaster of his?'

'Holder?' She smiled briefly. 'Yes, he did once. We was having supper one night and we got on talking about nicknames. And Wilf said he had a teacher they used to call Gripper, because his name was Holder, see? Wilf said this teacher was a smashing bloke, the lads 'ud do anything for him. Why'd you ask me about him?'

'Your lodger was found dead outside his back door,' Mallin answered. 'It seems he knew where Mr Holder lived. You don't know much about Dawson's friends. What about possible enemies?'

'None I ever heard of. He wasn't the sort

to make any, I would have said.'

'Right.' Mallin got up. 'We'd like to see his room. You will come with us, of course.'

'I'll just tell our Greta to keep an eye on the dinner...' She was back in a matter of seconds, ushering them up the stairs. Four doors faced on to a tiny landing. Mrs Saunders pointed to each in turn.

'My room, Greta's, bathroom and this is Wilf's.'

It was a small room. A single bed, a chair, a chest of drawers, a dressing table and a tiny wardrobe took up most of the space. The narrow windowsill held a row of books. Though the furniture was old, and chipped here and there, it shone with polish, and the bedclothes and dressing table runners were immaculate. Mrs Saunders was clearly a house-proud landlady.

She stood by the door while the CID men set to work. Mallin went across to the dressing table while Lee dealt with the chest of drawers and the wardrobe. Their hands moved quickly, purposefully.

The chest held only shirts, underwear, pyjamas, a selection of highly-coloured ties and socks. The wardrobe was crowded with what the late Wilfred Dawson probably called 'gear,' and there was a lower shelf which accommodated footwear.

'His toilet stuff's in the bathroom,' Mrs Saunders volunteered, 'and his working clothes I let him keep in the scullery.' Mallin nodded. Having found nothing of interest in the two long drawers of the dressing table, he was now tackling the couple of small ones at the top. Lee strolled across to watch.

The left-hand drawer was half-full of oddments – spare razor blades, studs, small tools of various sorts, a bottle of aspirin tablets amid a mass of other clutter. Mallin closed it after a brief glance. But the other small drawer was more productive. It held an untidy heap of papers which Mallin lifted out. He began to riffle through them quickly while Lee glanced at the books on the windowsill. They were mostly manuals on gardening and appeared to have been well read. The rest were paperbacks – westerns and thrillers.

'Right,' Mallin said. He had made two small piles of the papers, he put one of them back into the drawer and held up the other. 'I'll give you a receipt for these, Mrs Saunders. And, by the way, there's about forty pounds in this drawer, mostly singles. You'd better take charge of that lot. As for his stuff, it must stay where it is for now, we'll let you know what to do with it later. That his van outside?' She nodded. 'We found car keys on him, I'll send a man along to drive it away.'

Mrs Saunders began to murmur about an inquest and funeral.

'We'll be in touch,' Mallin promised her. 'Nothing for you to worry about.'

'Any luck with those papers, sir?' Lee asked as they drove away.

'Not a lot, Bonny, but they do tell us just a little more about him. Maybe, when you've sorted them out... Hell, I'm starving. Didn't have a proper breakfast this morning. Wednesday, isn't it? So the canteen lunch shouldn't be too bad.'

They had thick vegetable soup, steak and kidney pie with mashed and carrots, a jam roll and a large cup of strong tea.

'That's better,' Mallin said as he drained his cup. 'I could do with putting my feet up for twenty minutes, but no such luck. We'll sort out these papers, by which time Mr Trott'll be hollering for us.'

Detective Superintendent Trott looked up at them lugubriously as they entered his office.

'Got it cleared up, I hope? I've just had the ACC in here. He's busting a gut to get the

Death Rattler going. I persuaded him to hold off till you reported in.'

Grover, the Assistant Chief Constable, had recently sold the idea of a Mobile Murder Unit to the Benfield Watch Committee. This vehicle had now been supplied, to outside appearance a cross between a double-sized removal van and a millionaire's dormobile. Inside it had everything from a tele-communication system to an Aldis lamp, it carried generators for flood-, spot- and arc-lighting a complete office set-up and a detailed complement of maps, photographic and finger-printing equipment – in fact, everything the model cop might need to hunt a killer down. Its official designation was Mobile Murder Unit A, which seemed to suggest that the ACC, expecting homicide to break out on a large scale, had his eye on a future fleet of such vehicles. The existing one, which had not yet been put to use, had been nicknamed the Death Rattler by a police cadet and the designation had been enthusiastically taken up by the Force.

'We haven't got it cleared up, sir,' Mallin answered with some justifiable reproof. 'As for the MMUA you mentioned, which is supposed, I believe, to be set up at the scene of the crime, that just isn't on. Not unless you want Dainford Road blocked at both ends. But we've identified the body and got a bit of background.'

'Let's have it, then.' Trott listened, his cavernous face still drenched in gloom which failed to lighten when Mallin had finished. 'Feller seems to have been the biggest liar since Baron Munchausen. Everybody he met he told a different tale to, eh?' He flicked a fingernail at one of the papers Mallin had laid on his desk. 'Birth certificate says he was born here, in Benfield. Ah, driving licence. Clean one, anyway. What's this? Billhead from Langton and Wells, Scrap Metal Merchants, Royds Lane? I know that firm. Sound business they run, too. Payment for transport work done? I thought you said...?'

'I was quoting his landlady, sir, who must be a paragon for not nosing into her lodgers' private papers. And he must have trusted her, or she'd soon have found out that the so-called scrap metal business he said he owned was phony. Dawson merely did odd jobs for Langton and Wells, transporting stuff chiefly. I've rung the firm and they confirm this.'

'Yet he's registered as self-employed, sir,' Lee put in. 'I suppose that did something

48

for his ego.'

'Likely.' Trott sighed deeply. 'What about this alleged liaison with Mrs Whatsername – Norton?'

'Could be another tall story sir. I'll have it checked. And Lee's going along to that High Swing place this afternoon.'

'Ah. Belongs to Pelling, doesn't it?' Trott let his right hand close slowly into a fist. 'I've always said I'd retire happy if I could only nail that bird. Just once.' He cast up his eyes and made it sound like a supplication. Then he picked up a typed paper from his desk.

'PM report, this. Forensic dug a bullet out of the skull. From a .22 Walther PPK, they reckon. Gun used at a distance of three to five yards. Plenty of Walthers about, of course.' He looked up. 'There's only one method in a case like this – dig into the background. As far as I can see, we've got no choice. So keep the spades going, and fast!'

Outside the superintendent's room Mallin grunted, 'See you,' to Lee and strode heavily away towards his own office. Lee walked down to the ground floor, en route to what Mallin had called 'that High Swing place.' This was a discotheque with a dance floor attached, much frequented by the city's

49

teenagers. It was the type of establishment the police kept a casual, routine eye on, though in its six years of existence it had never given trouble. There was no suspicion of drug-trafficking there and if, as could be expected occasionally, a spot of bother blew up amongst the clients, it was jumped on instantly and the trouble-makers told to get out – and not to come back. Raymond Trent, who managed the place for its owner, Louis Pelling, was a decided 'square' in that respect. He believed in discipline for the young. As a result, his customers respected him.

The afternoon was overcast, with a hint of fog to come by nightfall. Carlton Street, Lee's objective, was less than five minutes' walk from HQ. Not worth bothering with a car.

As he stepped out along the pavement Lee thought, not of the High Swing, but of its owner. Louis Pelling ran three gambling clubs, a string of betting shops and a large and popular hotel just outside Benfield. Ten years previously, he had come to Benfield from London to manage one of the local cinemas, after a few months he had resigned and gone into other forms of entertainment. And he had rocketed, with apparent ease and certainly with celerity, to a big flat, one of a number he owned in the Amberley district, a white Mercedes-Benz and all the trimmings to match.

The suspicious police mind never feels easy when a man, with no evident capital nor backers, mushrooms as Pelling had done. Among the brass of the Benfield City Police it was held, quite firmly, that Pelling was on the crook, somehow, somewhere. The trouble was, such a conviction had never been substantiated, in spite of various whispers dropped into the ears of both uniformed and plainclothes men by normally trustworthy contacts, and duly passed on. There was nothing, just nothing, to connect Louis Pelling with those two wage snatches, the supermarket break-in, the series of antique silver thefts from private houses. And there should have been, according to those contacts. Yet tactful investigations had all shown up Louis Pelling and his affairs as whiter than white.

Carlton Street was in the centre of town, a narrow passage linking two of the main shopping thoroughfares. But its shops – jewellers, tailoring and women's clothing stores in the main – were sumptuously window-dressed and all expensive. In the middle of the street, at one side, the High Swing gleamed brightly on this dull afternoon, a neon sign winking above its entrance, which was outlined in coloured electric light bulbs. A small group of youths and girls lounged in the doorway, smoking and chattering. None of them took any notice of Lee as he mounted the shallow steps.

Inside, a thickly-carpeted foyer, also brightly lit, had a hotel-like reception desk facing the entrance. On either side of it were closed doors, from behind which came a complex mixture of pop music. The door on the left opened and a man came through; Lee caught a glimpse of couples on a dance floor, jerking agitatedly as they faced each other, for all the world as if they had been subjected to a giant-sized tin of itching powder.

The man walked to the back of the desk, leant his forearms on it and watched Lee's approach over the carpet. He was a smallish man, but chunkily-built, with a flat nose, a swarthy complexion and thick lips. Lee knew him as the manager of this place, one of Pelling's most trusted henchmen. He called himself Raymond Trent, though his Middle East appearance hardly suited the English name.

'Sergeant Lee, isn't it?' His voice was deep, faintly accented. The lips parted in a brief, white-toothed smile. 'And how's things coming with you, eh?'

'So-so, Mr Trent. Busy as usual, of course.' Lee brought out the photograph of Wilfred Dawson. 'Do you know this man?'

Trent studied the photograph carefully, then he looked up.

'Should I? Know him, I mean?'

'I'm just asking you if you do,' Lee said patiently.

'Well, now–' Trent broke off as a lad of seventeen or so, with a freckled face and gingery hair down to his shoulders, came in from the street and slouched up to the desk. 'What is it, Terry? Look, I'm busy.'

'I was only going to ask you, Mr Trent–'

'Save it till later.' Trent waved him away. The lad grimaced sulkily and wandered to one of the foyer walls where he began to study a Top Ten list of records. Trent said, 'Sorry about that, but some of these kids think they're lords of creation. Everything has to stop for them. Now, about this bloke.' He tapped the photograph. 'The face is familiar but I can't put a name to it. What blows, anyway?'

'He was found shot dead out Northfield

53

way this morning. We've been told he came here dancing quite frequently.'

'That'll be it, then. Why I know his face, I mean.'

'His name is Wilfred Dawson. Does that ring a bell?'

Trent shook his head. 'Hundreds of 'em come in here. As long as they behave themselves their names don't matter to me.'

'Can you tell me if he came alone, or with a girl friend, or as one of a crowd?'

'No idea, pal. He couldn't have been one of the every-nighters, that's all I can say. I've a group here – they call themselves The Roamers – who do the music bit every night, they might have noticed him but there's none of 'em here this afternoon. The old juke-box provides the sound for afternoon dancing. If I were you, I'd come back later.'

'So if I tell you that Wilfred Dawson had claimed he was a close friend of yours, you wouldn't agree?'

'I'd say, with all due respect seeing the poor bastard's copped it, that he was the biggest liar of this side of the Smoke.'

Lee nodded. 'Thanks. Mr Trent. I had to check how much you knew about him, if anything.'

'Sorry I couldn't help, Mr Lee.' As Lee turned away from the desk he saw the ginger-haired youth moving towards the main doorway. Trent called, 'Hey, Terry, I thought you wanted to see me?' The lad flung a scowl at him, shrugged and went hurriedly outside.

The mistiness of the afternoon was gathering under the street lamps now. Lee turned to his left at the bottom of the steps, back to HQ. The story Dawson had told Mrs Saunders and her daughter, that he was friendly with Trent, was obviously just another of his tall stories and entirely without foundation. In other words a wasted journey for Lee himself.

A voice said, from behind him, 'Hey, mister!' He turned his head and saw Terry, the ginger-haired youth, a pace or so to the rear. Lee stopped.

'Look.' Terry spoke quickly. 'I heard you asking Ray Trent about this Wilfred Dawson. And Ray said he didn't know him. Well, he's a bloody liar, see? Him and Dawson, they was right mates. I've seen Dawson, many a time, going into Ray's private office.'

'You wouldn't know what sort of business they did together?'

'Not a clue. I might be able to find

something out, though. It's Wednesday, and Mr Pelling – you know he owns the High Swing, I s'pose? – he always looks in between half nine and ten. I've got me this feeling that when he comes tonight, they'll get talking about Dawson.'

'And how would you be able to hear what they say?'

'I work at the Swing, nights. Sorta waiter. We serves drinks – all soft, of course – and snacks. From a kind of bar, like. I'm in charge of this. And then, when we close, I sweep up and all that.'

'I still don't see–'

'I'm telling yer, aren't I? Ray's office is just back of the wall behind the bar and there's this little hatch. I can open it a bit so's it isn't noticed from the office and when I sorta lean back and put my ear to it, I can hear quite well.'

'Suppose I ask you to do that, and you hear something I might like to know, what do you expect to get out of it?'

Terry shrugged. 'Oh, I dunno. A bit of me own back on Ray Trent, maybe. He can be a bloody swine to work for, y'know. I mean, mister, I'm skint. Three flamin' favourites in a row let me down. So I come here this afternoon, going to ask him if he'll sub me a coupla quid till Sat'day, when I get paid. But I know damn well the bastard wouldn't have. As I say, I'm skint.'

Lee grinned understandingly. 'You know who I am?'

'I know you're a policeman, like. 'Cos as I was going inta the Swing, some cat on the steps ses, "Hey, Terry, one of the pigs has just gone in there." Me, I don't use that sorta talk,' he added quickly.

Lee took out his wallet and extracted two pound notes from it.

'What's your full name – and your address, lad?'

'Terry Kershaw. I live at 14 Canal Road.' He eyed the notes greedily. Lee handed him one of them and put the other away.

'You close up at eleven – right? If you get anything, call in at Central Station. You'll know it, it's on your way home. Ask for Sergeant Lee. I'll be waiting there and if you have any gen for me, you'll get the other note, and maybe an extra one to go with it. Okay?'

'I'll be there, Mr Lee.' He turned on his heel and went slouching across the road while Lee continued his own way to his headquarters.

He was sitting in the CID officer, putting the finishing touches to the report of his day's activities, when WDC Radley came briskly in. Lee looked up at her.

'And what have you been doing with your afternoon? By your appearance, young Sylvia, I'd guess a couple of hours in a beauty parlour.'

'You're sweet, Sarge, even if you don't mean it.' Like most of the 'wopsies' on the Force, Sylvia had fallen, hopelessly, she knew, for Bonny Lee five seconds after she had met him. She guessed there must be a heart somewhere behind that super-handsome face and figure, but in her book it was made of specially-hardened granite. Ah, well, that was the way it went...

'Mr Mallin sent me to Dainford Way, Sarge, to talk to the Nortons' neighbours. Nobody at home on one side, but on the other – gosh, did I get an earful!'

She hung up the light coat she was wearing and sat down opposite him.

'A Mrs Tillotson. Small, stringy, fiftyish. Spiteful, too. The Tillotsons had some trouble recently with the Nortons – some long tale she told me to do with what fence belonged to who, so I put a twenty-five per cent discount on what she told me about Mrs Norton. She swears that lady was having an affair with Dawson – "Misbehav-

58

ing herself frequently" was how she put it. She, Mrs Tillotson, had clearly been keeping an eye lifting on next door.

'She said on the days Dawson came there, he only worked outside in the mornings and spent the afternoons in the house, when the daily woman had gone. Then cleared off in his van before her husband got home. Of course, she'd never seen or heard anything definite, trust Mrs Norton to watch that – I'm quoting, of course – but she'd watched Mrs Norton wave Dawson off in his van a few times, and by the look on her face, well, any woman could tell what they'd been up to.'

Lee had listened with his usual courteous attention. He was trying to work out a sum in his head. Add seventy-five percent of Mrs Tillotson's story to what Mrs Carr, the Nortons' daily woman, had said about Dawson, add also that Dawson himself had claimed, to his landlady, that he could do what he liked at the Nortons', subtract Dawson's propensity for lying and then put on Mrs Norton's faint when she heard of her gardener's death, and what was the final result? He didn't know, and there was no answer book from which he could crib the solution.

'Did Mrs Tillotson have anything to say about Mr Norton?' he asked.

Sylvia reflected a moment. 'Only that it was time somebody told him what was going on. D'you think, Sarge, that he did find out and plug Dawson in a fit of uncontrollable rage and jealousy, as they say?'

'I think we could both do with a cup of tea, Sylvia. So, if you would be good enough to direct those slim feet canteenwards...'

When she had gone, he began to consider Norton, the man whom none of them had yet seen. A quick interview would sweep up that corner, anyway. He found the number of the Benfield Wire Rope and Cable Company in Saville Street and called it. A switchboard operator said she would get Mr Norton's office for him.

A second female voice, crisply business-like, announced its owner as the managing director's secretary and asked how she could be of service. Lee identified himself. The voice at once became less formal, more human.

'Ah, Sergeant, no doubt this is in connection with Mr Norton's gardener? Or, to be precise, late gardener? Yes, he told me about it – Mrs Norton rang him, you see. He said you people might possibly want a word with him and that he'd hold himself at your disposal. He's free now, as a matter of fact.'

'I'll be with you in ten minutes. No–' Lee remembered his cup of tea – 'better make that twenty.' The secretary said, 'Quite all right,' so, exactly eighteen minutes later, Lee's Viva was nosing into a parking slot at the works in Saville Street where it had been directed by the gateman. Following further instructions, Lee went through a handsome portico into the main building, found a lift which took him to the third floor and to the secretary's office. She proved to be a well-built, attractive young woman with coppery glints in her brown hair and green eyes which took him in appreciatively. 'Mr Norton is expecting you,' she said, and went before him to an inner door with 'Managing Director – Julian Norton' across its upper panel.

Julian Norton was middle-aged, dark-haired, short in stature and running to fat in face and body. He rose, somewhat stiffly, to greet his visitor.

'Sit down, Mr Lee. This is a dreadful business. It seems to have shaken my wife up severely, but her nerves are never in the best of condition, and, of course, she knew

Dawson well.'

'I understand he was your gardener for two years?'

'Correct. I was unlucky enough to get a spinal injury, which still troubles me, incidentally. The doctors ordered no gardening, which nearly broke my heart, as it's always been my hobby. The place had got into an awful mess while I was in hospital, I simply had to get some help. Dawson turned up in response to my advertisement, I interviewed him and took him on. He wasn't what I'd call a top-class gardener, but then, my standards are high. However, needs must, you know. He kept the place more or less in order.'

'I've seen your garden, sir. I would hardly have thought there was enough work there to keep a man busy three days a week.'

Norton shrugged. 'You know what these chaps are. They don't sweat their guts out. And I've always felt I must give Dawson a certain amount of latitude, for had he left us I mightn't have found another man to take his place.'

'You wouldn't see much of him yourself?'

'Very little. He'd always gone when I reached home.' He grinned widely. 'But I heard plenty about him from my wife. She became quite friendly with him, was always talking about him. I got the impression he was a bit of a boaster and I warned her not to believe everything he said, but he seemed to do her good in some way. She was always more relaxed, less strung up, on the days when he'd been.'

'You'd no objection to this friendship, of course?'

Now Norton laughed aloud. 'Good God, no, Sergeant! Why should I? I know what's in your mind, but any idea of that sort is ridiculous! Why, she's old enough to have been his mother!' He drew his face into solemn lines. 'I was extremely sorry to learn of his death. And how I'll ever replace him, as a gardener, I just can't imagine!'

Chapter Four

'I honestly can't see Norton as a madly-jealous killer,' Lee told Mallin and Trott in the superintendent's office. 'If he had any reason to shoot Dawson, my bet is it wasn't because he thought his gardener was playing around with Mrs Norton.'

'So we cross him off the list of possible suspects?' Trott suggested. 'And take it that the fact Dawson was found dead only a street away from the Nortons' is pure coincidence?'

Mallin nodded his large head ponderously. 'I'd go along with that, sir. I favour the theory that Dawson was in some sort of serious trouble and went to Holder, his former schoolmaster, for advice or possibly help. There are absolutely no grounds either, to imagine Holder himself shot Dawson last night and then 'accidentally discovered the body this morning. I'll warrant he would have had more difficulty than Norton in getting hold of a Walther PPK to do the job with.'

'I've had all the known and suspected

64

gunmen on our patch checked,' Trott said. 'And every Benfield gunsmith. None of them have sold a Walther for several years.' He picked up a biro and began to fiddle with it. 'We've done everything I can think of and we've got nowhere.' His mantle of gloom was sitting firmly on his shoulders again.

'There's just the possibility,' Lee said, 'that I'll get something from this Kershaw lad tonight.'

'Yes,' Trott admitted. 'Dawson seems to have been a pretty hefty liar all round, but when he told his landlady he was a friend of Trent, it was Trent who lied when he said that wasn't true. Or so says your pal Kershaw, Lee.'

'We'll see about that, sir, when and if he calls in here on his way home tonight. I'll be back in good time to receive him.'

Trott took the hint. 'Yes, we've all had a long day. We can knock off now with justification. And good luck with your grasser, Sergeant.'

Lee drove to his top-floor flat in Rossington Court. It was an expensive 'pad' for a man on CID Sergeant's pay but a well-invested legacy from an aunt, plus careful budgeting, made it possible for him to maintain a home where he had only himself to consider and where he could find the peace and solitude he needed after the rushed hurly-burly of his working days. Though he had never considered himself as a born bachelor, unmarried status suited him very well. For the present, anyway. He was young, content with his job. Plenty of time to think of marriage and all that...

He showered in the tiny bathroom, washing away the physical grime and the mental frustrations of the day. He cooked himself a light but satisfying meal, switched the television on and watched, as he ate. He washed up, then settled down with the evening paper he had bought on his way home.

Golding, the police PR officer, had released the facts of Wilfred Dawson's death, on Trott's say-so, in time for the Benfield Evening Chronicle to make a front page story of it. The Holders had obviously had a busy day, too. Their photographs and a shot of the back of the house with a large white arrow pointing into the porch, were accompanied by a long interview with William Holder which told the public nothing more than they had already read in the headlines of the story. The report ended with the announcement that the police were treating the case as one of homicide, but that Detective Inspector Mallin, in charge of the field work of the investigation, had not been available for comment.

Lee grinned as he turned to the sports section. Mallin was hardly ever available for comment. He saw to that. He hated personal publicity like a hole in the head.

At a quarter past ten Lee went down to the flats' garage and got his car out again. The night staff at Central were settling down to the 'graveyard' spell of duty when he arrived. The station sergeant looked at him with some surprise.

'Hullo, Bonny! You got a sudden break on this Dawson job?'

'Nothing like that, Jim. I've a young chap coming to see me, soon after eleven. Meanwhile, I'll clear up a bit of paper work. Send him in to me when he arrives, will you?'

He accepted the inevitable offer of a mug of tea and took it into the CID office. As he completed the filling in of the last of six complicated information forms, he glanced up at the clock. It showed fourteen minutes past eleven.

He stretched, got up and went back to the main office counter. He stood there, chatting with the station sergeant, until half past eleven. There was no sign of Terry Kershaw.

'Changed his mind, most likely,' the station sergeant commented. 'They often do. Decide they won't get mixed up with nasty policemen, after all.'

'I'd have betted on this one turning up, Jim. He was mad keen on the dough I offered him.' Lee hesitated, and then, 'I'll just have a look outside. Maybe he got the arrangement wrong and expected to meet me in the street.'

But Carlton Street showed no signs of Terry Kershaw. A patrol car, however, was standing at the pavement edge between him and the High Swing where an alley, narrow and badly-lit, separated Louis Pelling's property from that of a furrier.

Lee saw that one of the two patrolmen was seated at the wheel of the car, the other was just about to get in beside his mate. Lee shouted, 'Hi! Hang on a minute, Gill!' and the man turned and waited expectantly.

Lee hurried towards the car. The patrolman grinned.

'You're too late for the show, Sarge. It's all over, everything done and dusted.'

'Show? What's all this, then?'

'Kid got roughed up in the alley yonder. Fellow going by heard him groaning, had a look-see. Dialled three nines in the call-box yonder and Young and me were sent here. Nobody around except the bloke who'd rung in, and he'd seen nothing. Kid was barely conscious, looked to be hurt bad. He'd been done over all right, I've seen too many jobs like that in the past five years to be mistaken. Young called an ambulance, it's just gone this minute, to St Aidan's. He was too bad even to give up his name, anyway, I doubt if he knew it, the state he was in.'

Lee shrugged off the grip of the cold hand which had clutched his heart. 'Description?'

'Seventeen, eighteen, I'd say. Gingery hair, fuzzy, shoulder-length. Slim built, freckled face where it wasn't all blood.'

'Right. St Aidan's, you said? I know who he is, I'll attend to the rest of it.' He decided to explain further; these two would be wondering why he had stopped them driving away. 'Matter of fact, he was due to contact me tonight. Reckoned he had something for me.' He shrugged. 'You can get on your way now, lads.'

He went back to Central, yawned through another twenty minutes to give Casualty at St Aidan's time to do their initial job and then rang the hospital from the station. After some delay the voice of a cheerful-sounding houseman answered.

'Dr Castleton here. You're police, I understand. And it's re the ginger-haired lad I've just been examining. Have no fears, he isn't going to die. Though he'll feel very sorry for himself for some days. Extensive bruising about the face and head and a couple of ribs fractured. Want his name and address? We found them in his wallet.'

'Terence Kershaw, Canal Road?'

'That's it. And now you're going to ask me if he can be interviewed. The answer's no, pal, not tonight. He's already under sedation. You might try your luck tomorrow morning, though.'

Lee thanked him, promised to let the lad's people know. The station sergeant said he'd send a patrol car to 14 Canal Road. The Kershaws would be told that Terry had had a slight accident on his way home from work and had been detained at St Aidan's for the night. There was no cause for worry, and he could be visited in the morning.

It had turned one o'clock when Lee wriggled down between the sheets. He was asleep in seconds flat.

At nine the following morning, after a phone call to Mallin to get the go-ahead, Lee stepped out of the frantic rush of the city streets into the placid atmosphere of St

Aidan's Hospital. There was plenty of movement here, too, but it was controlled, purposeful. He was directed to a ward where a nurse asked him to wait in an anteroom while she had a word with Sister.

Lee nodded to the two people also waiting in the room. One was a small middle-aged woman with a lined anxious face who fiddled unceasingly with her handbag and umbrella. The other, a tall willowy girl who carried a briefcase, sat by her side, relaxed and perfectly still. She had smooth auburn hair and a very fair skin, a pretty girl by any standard. Lee took a chair and remarked pleasantly that it was a mild morning for the time of year. He might have unblocked the outflow of a dam. The older woman took a deep breath and let go.

'I don't know what you think, mister, but I reckon it's high time the police did something about all these louts as go about beating up innocent folks! You'd think, in this day and age, a place like Benfield 'ud be safe enough to—'

The girl with her spoke quietly, firmly.

'Just take it easy, Mum. Give it a rest. Other people have their troubles besides us, you know.' She smiled at Lee and there was apology in her expression. She had a pleasant voice, which carried only a trace of the Benfield accent. As she had turned her head towards him recognition came. He knew who these two were.

'I think you're waiting to see Terry Kershaw, aren't you?'

The elder woman stared at him, her hands still now.

'We are. Me and me daughter Marion here. But how did you know that?'

'I'm Detective Sergeant Lee, and Terry was to have seen me last night after the High Swing closed–'

He got no further. 'I was sitting up for him, like as I allus do. And worrying because he was so late. Then this policeman come and said he'd bin in an accident, but I hadn't to worry and he'd be okay today. So this morning–'

The girl cut in neatly again. 'I rang the hospital here and was told he could be visited, that he'd had a beating-up in the street last night but wasn't in any kind of danger. That, in fact, he'd probably be discharged later today. And that if he wished, we could see him this morning.'

Lee nodded. 'I'm here myself for that purpose. And I'm going to ask you a favour. I'm a very busy man, I'd like to see him before you do. I promise you I won't be more than a few minutes.'

He got quickly to his feet as a ward sister came into the room. She looked sternly at him but he held out his warrant card and she said, 'Ah, yes, of course. This way, please.' She turned and went out without a word to the waiting women.

Lee followed her along a ward to where Terry Kershaw was sitting bolt upright in bed and looking extremely sorry for himself. His face was swollen in patches of red and blue and one eye was almost closed. There was a bandage round his skull, the fingers of his left hand were also bandaged. At Lee's approach his puffed-up lips set mulishly and his brows drew together in a frown.

There was an empty bed on one side of him, on the other, a white-haired man lay staring at the ceiling. The sister jerked her head at the man.

'He's completely deaf, won't hear a word you say.'

She whisked off and Lee drew up a chair and sat down.

'Well, Terry, you remember me – Detective Sergeant Lee? So who did this to you?'

Young Kershaw's good eye was directed ceilingwards.

'Don't know,' he muttered. 'Just got set on, that's all.'

'How many were there?'

'Can't tell you.'

'Can't? Or won't? Come on, now. You left work as usual, you were on your way to Central to see me. What happened then?'

'Look, I don't know. I don't know nothing. I'm saying nothing.'

'Did you pick up any information for me, as you hoped to do?'

'No.' The eye turned angrily upon Lee. 'See, mister, I've got one hell of a headache. Me ribs hurt and I feel rotten all over. Why don't you leave me alone? I got nothing to say to you.'

'Okay, Terry. We'll wait till you're fit again, and talk then, eh?'

Kershaw sighed. 'You must be deaf or something. I'm telling you nothing. Can't you dig that?'

Lee stood up. 'If that's the way it is...' He took out his wallet, slid two pound notes from it and held them between his fingers.

'So I don't owe you these, after all? You didn't even try to get that information for me?'

'I did, though. But...' He shook his head. 'I got nothing to say.'

74

Lee put the notes on top of the locker by the bed. 'Your mother and sister are waiting to see you. I hope you get fit soon.'

He walked out of the ward with a word of thanks to the sister. Outside the swinging glass doors Mrs Kershaw was waiting impatiently, alone. She grabbed Lee's arm.

'You've been talking to him, haven't you? I could see you through these doors. That sister said you were a copper.'

'It was my job to try and find out who Terry's attackers were, Mrs Kershaw. Unfortunately, he was unable to tell me... What happened to your daughter?'

'She couldn't stop. She's at the university, you see.' A note of pride crept into Mrs Kershaw's voice. 'And seeing Terry isn't all that bad, and time was getting on and she didn't want to be late for a lecture...' She turned to point along the corridor, where Lee now saw the auburn-haired girl standing in a little group by the lift doors. He said a hurried farewell to Mrs Kershaw and hastened, long-striding, towards the lift. He was the last in when the lift arrived.

Last in, first out. He moved to one side in the vestibule, then went forward quickly as the girl stepped out and turned towards the

75

entrance door.

'Excuse me, Miss Kershaw. I'm Detective Sergeant Lee and I'd appreciate a word with you.'

She swung round and smiled at him.

'Oh! You're the policeman who jumped the queue to see my brother. Did he tell you what you wanted to know?'

'Terry's not talking, Miss Kershaw. Not to me, at any rate. I think he's too scared. Now, I know you're in a hurry to get to the university, your mother told me so, but my car's outside and I'll run you along there. We can talk on the way.'

She laughed, and Lee liked the trilling sound of it. 'Sergeant, I'll come clean. We were assured that Terry wasn't dangerously hurt, I know my mother will slop and sentimentalise all over him as soon as she sees him, and I just couldn't face that. So I made a lying excuse and left. My first lecture today isn't for an hour yet.'

'So we could sit in my car and talk, Miss Kershaw?'

'My name's Marion, Sergeant. Lead the way.'

She was self-possessed without being too come-hither, he thought. Which was as well. He didn't go for girls of twenty, even beautiful ones. Marion Kershaw could claim that rating.

She duly admired the Viva de Luxe before she settled in beside him. Lee had hardly shut his door when she began to speak.

'I guess I know what this is all about, Sergeant. You want to discover who Terry's attackers were, and he won't tell you. Right? Well, it's no use asking me, of course. I haven't the least idea about that.'

'Terry won't talk because he daren't. I'm convinced of it. He's probably been told he'll get double what he got last night, and more, if he talks to us. And he was supposed to see me last night after his work.'

'Which means he has some sort of knowledge he shouldn't, in his attackers' opinion.'

'It's a sound theory. But I want that knowledge. Now, you know Terry better than I do. Is he likely to remain scared? Or, when he feels a good deal fitter than he does now, will he open up?'

She ran a slim finger along the imitation-leather briefcase she held upright in her lap.

'You're not asking me to work on him for you, are you?'

'By no means. I'm merely trying to plan ahead.'

77

Her finger stilled and she half-turned to face him.

'I think you'd better know the family set-up. My father pushed off and left us nine years ago. I was eleven and Terry was eight. He wasn't much of a catch, my father, a compulsive gambler who had other weaknesses, too. I'm afraid Terry is like him in many ways.' She caught her breath in a small sigh. 'Anyway, I did pretty well at school – and poor old Terry didn't – and what with hard work on mother's part, and, I can claim, some on mine, well, I'm studying for a degree in modern languages now. And since he left school, Terry has drifted from one unskilled job to another. At present he is – or was until today – a sort of general dogsbody at the High Swing. But you probably know that?'

'Yes. I had to go there yesterday, a routine visit in connection with a case I'm working on. I was hoping to get some information from the manager, Raymond Trent, about one of his customers. Trent claimed he didn't know this man at all well. Your brother was present and later made himself known to me and offered to get me the information I was seeking.'

'For money, of course? I know Terry. But I

78

haven't answered your question yet, have I? Will Terry talk later on? The definite answer to that is no, if he's been well and truly scared. Terry loves Terry. He values his skin above all things.'

Lee shrugged. 'Don't we all?' He leaned forward to switch on the car's engine. This chat with Marion Kershaw seemed unlikely to be more than time-wasting.

But she said quickly, 'Just a minute, Sergeant. You said you wanted information about a man who frequents the High Swing. It wouldn't be Dawson, by any chance? The man who was found shot yesterday morning?'

'It was. You know something about Dawson?'

'No. It was just that when he read about the death in the evening paper last night, before he went to work, Terry said Dawson was a great friend of Raymond Trent. He said that Dawson and Trent and James Venner – do you happen to know Doctor Venner?'

'I don't, Marion.'

'He's a Ph D. He's in the Department of Sociology at the university. Very, very Left Wing. The complete hippie type.' She shuddered distastefully. 'I don't know him very well, I don't want to. But he's ace-high with some of the students – the sort who say you've got to smash all the existing systems down in order to live the full, free life – but you'll have heard all that clap-trap before, I'm sure.'

'Yes, and I don't like it, either. But you were going to tell me something about this Venner and the High Swing.'

'Only that according to Terry, he's a frequent visitor there. And that Terry had seen him talking to Trent and Dawson.'

'Mr Pelling is the owner of that place. Did Terry ever mention him in connection with Dawson and Venner?'

'No… No, I'm sure he didn't. Look, I'm not getting Terry into any sort of trouble talking to you like this? He's weak and an awful nit in some ways, but he isn't any sort of criminal type.'

'I think I could have told you that, Marion. A policeman gets a certain instinct about these things.' Lee looked at his watch. 'We'll have to break this up. Time's getting on. I'll drop you at the university–'

'No need for that, thanks.' She was out of the car like a flash. 'I like a walk in the mornings.'

She gave him a warm smile and was gone.

Chapter Five

'And where the flaming hell,' Mallin demanded, 'have you been? Nearly ten o'clock, and you just turn in. Of course, it could be you've solved that Dawson case, I suppose?'

'Not quite, sir. Though I've been working on it.'

Mallin listened to his sergeant's report. 'Doesn't get us very far, though,' he grunted. 'You seem to have some proof this fellow Trent's a liar – another one! – and you think the attack on Kershaw has some connection with what he promised to tell you last night. I suppose you'd better follow that up. But that High Swing spot won't be open until this afternoon... Might be worthwhile having a word with Venner, though, on the lines we're still digging into Dawson's background, interviewing everybody who knew him.'

'I take it you'll see Venner yourself, sir?'

Mallin shook his head. 'Not this morning. Mr Trott and I have a conference with the

Chief at half-past ten. You go along and get hold of Venner if you can. Luckily, apart from Dawson, we've nothing very urgent on the books. What there is, Danby, Sylvia Radley and Jones can look after.'

So Lee drove to the university after all, was directed by a traffic warden to one of the car parks and walked back to the main entrance, up a wide flight of steps and through swing doors into a foyer beyond which was a high-ceilinged, pillared hall, extensive and nobly proportioned.

There was a porter's office at one side of the foyer, Lee showed his warrant card and received directions for the Department of Sociology. This was part of a huge, ugly concrete building, and he pushed through the inevitable swing doors and found a glassed-in cubbyhole with a man in charge who pointed to a lift.

'Third floor, you want. That's Sociology. You'll see the sec'tary's room opposite you as you come out.'

The secretary proved to be an attractive young woman who said that Dr Venner was engaged with a student but should be free at any moment. She gave Lee a chair, but he had hardly seated himself when a door across the secretary's room, with a plague announcing James Venner MA Ph D, opened, and a weedy-looking young man with long greasy hair and a scrubby beard came out. He wore scuffed shoes, dirty jeans and a dingy polo-necked green sweater. He turned his head and shouted into the room he had just left.

'I still say you're wrong, Jimmy, you git! What you want to do, mate, is to get your bloody brains working, if you've got any! You argue like a bloody pregnant schoolgirl!'

A roar of laughter from Dr Venner's room was the only answer he received. He came forward, grinning at the secretary.

'Just told the old bastard off, I have. Time somebody did. Hey, sweetheart, how about you and me having a tumble sometime? I rather fancy you, you know.'

The young woman looked up at him and said quietly, 'Just close the door when you go out, Mr Harriman.'

'Oh, not in the mood today, eh? Well, I can wait.' As he passed by Lee's chair the CID man caught the stink of unwashed clothes and filthy skin. The secretary got up as the door closed.

'They're not all like that, you know,' she said, and went into the other room, leaving the door open. Lee heard the murmur of her voice, then a man answered her.

'But must I, Anne?' The tones were petulant. 'I mean, one of the pigs! It's too much to ask at this time of day, surely?' She spoke again and then Lee heard, 'Oh, all right. Let's get it over.'

Ushered in, Lee saw a large room with a window overlooking the campus, shelves and cases of books, various chairs scattered around. A big desk occupied the centre of the room and behind it sat a short, stout man with a fuzzball of light brown hair standing out around his head, bearded cheeks, shaven chin and upper lip. Lee put his age in the middle thirties. He wore a belted blouse in a vivid patchwork of colour, a heavy gilt chain with a medallion hung round his neck. His desk was cluttered with papers and books and he didn't rise when Lee entered.

'Find him a chair, Anne.' He had a deep voice which didn't seem to go with his lack of inches. Lee turned to help the secretary to wheel up a heavy armchair with a low seat. He said pleasantly, 'You have my name, sir. My business with you shouldn't take long.'

Dr Venner picked up a pencil and began to tap his front teeth with it. They were small teeth with spaces between them.

'I suppose,' he said with a grin which had nothing of amusement nor friendliness in it, 'that under the present rotten system people like you are, to a certain extent, necessary. Future generations will marvel that we put up with you, paid taxes to support you.'

Lee's answering grin was entirely urbane.

'I am also a taxpayer, sir. In a small way I support students in this university – and their mentors. Which puts us about level, doesn't it? Likewise, we are both busy men, you and I. It's my duty to ask you a few questions.'

'But not mine to answer them. However, let's hear 'em.'

'Very good, sir. You will no doubt have seen in the papers of the unexplained death of Wilfred Dawson. I am given to understand you knew him.'

The teeth-tapping began again. Through it, Venner said, 'I never read newspapers. My work is not connected with mass media... Dawson... One of my students, perhaps? I don't seem to dig...'

'You know the High Swing in Carlton Street, sir?'

'Ah!' Venner dropped the pencil on his desk. '*That* Dawson! Why, of course! Did

85

you say he was dead? I had no idea.'

'He was found shot through the brain in Dainford Road yesterday morning. We're trying to make a search into his background, talking to all the people who knew him. In an endeavour to find his killer, of course.'

'So, I presume, having found nothing of value among his – er – underworld contacts, you come to me?'

Lee concealed a sudden surge of interest. How well did you know Dawson, sir?'

The gaudily-covered shoulders moved in protest. 'See, comrade, will you cut out the sirring – I don't go for it. You address me as Jim, which is my name, a request I make to everyone I know.'

Lee, who had no intention of complying, merely nodded.

'I'd like an answer to my question, if you please.'

'Ah, yes. How well did I know Dawson? I met him – oh, some half-dozen times at the Swing. I have made that place part of a field study area I am working on. I am researching on the habits, the language, dress and motivations of the sixteen to twenty-one age group. I talk to the cats and the dollies who frequent such places. All in the cause of science, of course.'

'Dawson was twenty-nine. Rather out of the age limits you set yourself.'

'Yes, but he was a special case, inasmuch as he was a compulsive talker, though he failed to get the following, the group-nucleus of weaker types, which normally are attracted to such a person. This characteristic, the flowing in towards and the eventual submission to a fellow human who seems to possess the magic – to them – of the spoken word, is a norm in most societies. Dawson seemed to me to be unable to make this leadership rating. I found it interesting to try to discover exactly what quality he lacked in that respect. I was not wholly successful there.'

'You mentioned the underworld in connection with Dawson. In what way did he talk about it?'

'That he was well in, as he put it, with various gentlemen who, one gathered, were definitely not friends of the fuzz. That if anybody wanted a job done, he, Dawson, could put him in touch with the slickest operator in town. One gathered that nobody robbed a bank, raped a child nor cut the throat of a mother-in-law without asking Dawson's advice as to the best way to set about it. One didn't believe him, naturally.'

Venner sat forward and spoke quite eagerly. 'It could be, you know, that there I have inadvertently put my finger on the answer to the problem I mentioned just now. Was it because he was such an obvious liar that he failed to move into the leadership bracket? Can we postulate that even the moronic stratum of society instinctively recognizes a liar for what he is, and rejects him?'

'Outside my field of knowledge, I'm afraid. Did you have anything at all to do with Dawson besides meeting him at the High Swing?'

'Good God – if I may be permitted to refer to a non-existing being – no.' He drew a sheet of paper towards him and began to write. 'Assuming my theory could be correct, what examples have we in former societies of what we may term, for want of a better phrase, the compulsive liar syndrome? There's a passing reference in Lowenstein, I seem to recollect...'

Lee got up quietly and, his going clearly unmarked, left Venner to his speculations.

Complete waste of time, he thought sourly as he emerged on to the campus and took a deep lungful of air. The atmosphere in Venner's room, which had nothing to do with its air-conditioning, had, to Lee, been tainted with something to which he couldn't put a name, but which he hadn't liked one little bit. It had also left a very nasty taste in his mouth.

A man was sweeping up leaves in the campus. Lee went up to him.

'Good morning. Is there anywhere around I could get a cup of coffee?'

'Sure, sir.' The man leaned on his broom. 'See that door, up them steps? Go right to the end of the corridor inside, down some more steps as you'll find there, and you'll see one of these snack bars facing you. They'll fix you up there.'

The snack bar took up half the length of one side of an extensive café-like area, crowded with small tables with four chairs at each. The place was more than three-quarters full of customers and Lee noted, as he waited his turn at the counter, that these were by no means all students. It was obviously used by the general public of the university, from teaching staff to cleaners. He received his coffee, paid for it at a cash desk and, as he turned to seek a table, caught the eye of Marion Kershaw, who, seated with a young man in a corner by a window, was waving at Lee, beckoning him over. He made his way across to her.

The young man, who was tall, stockily-built, with weather-tanned features that were only just short of handsome, got up to pull out a chair for Lee. The CID man looked at him, then thrust out a hand.

'Well, what d'you know? Roger Ineson, by the powers!'

'And it's grand to meet you again, Mr Lee.' Roger pumped his hand heartily. 'How's the right cross these days? Anyway sit down. I–'

'Just a minute!' Marion pleaded. 'I didn't know you two were acquainted. I saw you come in, Mr Lee, and mentioned to Roger I'd met you this morning. He said, "Let's get him over here," but I'd no idea you'd met this hulking brute before. What did you run him in for?'

'I didn't, though I'd every reason to, the last time we were in each other's company. Assault and battery, the committing of grievous bodily harm with intent, obstructing a police officer.'

Roger grinned. 'I ought to have got that points decision, you know. It all depended on the last round, and if you hadn't been mean enough to close up my left eye–'

'Oh!' Marion said. 'I've got it. Boxing, eh?'

'University versus Benfield Police,' Lee

replied. 'Light-heavyweight class. But it was a good scrap, Roger. I'll admit my legs were wobbling all over the place when the final bell went.'

'Don't say you're going through it all again, blow by blow,' Marion remonstrated. 'I'm curious to know what you're doing here, Mr Lee.'

'Routine enquiries on a certain case. And that's all you'll get out of me, young woman, except to say I've just had a brief interview with Dr James Venner.'

'Him?' Roger grimaced. 'Pity there isn't a spittoon around here. I feel I could use it.'

'You know him well?'

'No, not in the way you mean. I'm doing Agriculture – final year. So our paths don't cross, praise be. But I've heard plenty about him. Absolutely student power, red revolution, smash down authority, carve up the Establishment – that's what he preaches, and you'd be surprised, Mr Lee, at the number of brainless twits in this university who think he's God Almighty. That makes him a danger, you know. They – the Vice Chancellor and his crowd – should kick him out of here. But they daren't. They're a gutless lot.'

'Roger,' Marion observed, 'is no progressive, you note, Mr Lee. He's hopelessly out of date. He believes in discipline, hard work, decent manners. That's why I like him,' she added with a smile.

'It stands to sense–' Roger cut himself short, then went on again. 'You can't help hearing things – in the Union, at the bars, in the refectory. Personally, I think Venner's a menace. I think he has some idea – it sounds a bit way-out, I know – of taking over this place. He's got quite a big following, and not only among the students.' He grinned. 'You'd better not quote me, Mr Lee, until I've done my finals, at any rate. You still in training?'

They fell easily into boxing chat until Marion looked at the clock over the bar and said that, fascinated as she was by this talk of in-fighting and the best way to tackle a southpaw, she must tear herself away for a tutorial. Roger, too, admitted he ought to be strolling over to hear Prof Elston waffle through his usual Thursday morning lecture, and the party split up.

On the way to retrieve his car, Lee thought about Venner. A Napoleon type, or just a big-mouth blatterer? He couldn't decide. And, fortunately, he didn't have to. He drove out of the park, thinking of all the people he had met in this Dawson case. William Holder,

Dawson's old schoolmaster, on whose premises the body was found, the Nortons, Dawson's employers, the Saunders, where he lodged, Raymond Trent and the Kershaw family. And now Venner.

Julian Norton apart, who amongst those might possibly have a reason to put a bullet into Dawson's brain? The answer seemed to be none of them. Not even Norton. Lee couldn't see him as a revenger of wifely infidelities. And it was hard to accept the idea of Mrs Norton and Dawson as lovers. She had been foolish, perhaps, in becoming too familiar with her gardener, and people would talk... But there had been no atmosphere of guilt nor of desolate grief in the way Mrs Norton had received the news of Dawson's death. True, she had thrown a faint, but that had not been significant in Lee's opinion. Nor in Tom Mallin's, either, he knew. Though you could never be sure with women.

Canal Road, where the Kershaws lived, was less than a mile east of the university. It was possible that, having visited her son, Mrs Kershaw would spend the rest of the morning in town shopping and so forth. Or she may have gone straight home. It was worth a try.

She recognized him the instant she opened the door of the small house to his knock.

'You're the policeman as went in to see our Terry.' Her hand flew to her mouth. 'Here, he isn't gone and got suddenly worse?'

'Oh, no, Mrs Kershaw, nothing like that. I'm Detective Sergeant Lee and I'm trying to find out who it was who set on Terry last night. He didn't seem inclined to talk to me – of course, he's still feeling a bit under the weather – but I expect he told you all about it?' He used his ingratiating smile on her.

She looked at him steadily for a few moments, then she said, 'Will you come in? I'd like to talk to you.'

The sitting room into which she led him was neat and tidy, though every item of its furniture, except perhaps the television set, spoke of long residence between those four walls. Mrs Kershaw switched on an old-fashioned electric fire and invited Lee to use the settee. She sat in a small chair facing him.

'Terry had a real beating-up.' She spoke with a note of accusation as if it were entirely Lee's fault. He nodded sympathetically.

'I was glad to know his injuries aren't serious, Mrs Kershaw. Though that's not much consolation to him, I'm sure. He wouldn't talk to me, you know. But no doubt he was more forthcoming to you?'

'That's the trouble, he wasn't. All he said was he didn't know who'd done it, nor why, and would I leave him alone and stop worrying him about it? But you can tell me this. Is he in any sort of bother with the police?'

'None at all, I can assure you of that.' He went on to tell her of his meeting with Terry the previous day and of the appointment they had arranged.

'I think it may be possible,' he ended, 'that Terry did pick up some information for me, that somebody found this out and persuaded him, if I can put it that way, not to hand it on.'

'But why should he want to get mixed up with you at all?'

'Because he was going to be paid for it, Mrs Kershaw.'

She was silent for a full minutes, her hands moving restlessly in her lap. Then she spoke wearily.

'Kids – they can make life hard... Of course, he's just like his dad was. Marion, now, she's as different as can be. Got brains and works hard. 'Terry' – she shrugged –

'can't keep a job. Oh, I dunno!' Then a spark of life came into her voice. 'But it isn't all his fault. 'What's bred in the bone, like they say. He's a good boy at heart. He wouldn't do anything that was really wrong.'

'I'm sure he wouldn't. Tell me, did he like his job at the High Swing?'

'Not all that much. But it kept his morning free, y'see, and he allus did like to lie abed late. He couldn't stand his boss, though. That Trent. On'y yesterday Terry was on about chucking up there. I ses to him, "You stick it a bit longer, son. Never was a job yet where the boss was all that good."'

'What had he got against Trent, exactly?'

'Oh, I dunno. The way he was treated mostly, like a dog, he said it was. 'But I'll get me own back on him one day, you'll see,' he used to say.'

She sighed, then pressed her lips together. Lee saw he wouldn't get anything more out of her. He got up.

'Try and persuade Terry, when he comes out of hospital, to have a chat with me, Mrs Kershaw. It would be far better for him if he did.'

She also rose to see him out. 'I'll do what I can, Sergeant.'

Chapter Six

The top brass conference was still functioning when Lee got back to HQ. He glanced through a couple of reports which had been put on his desk and then proceeded to type out one of his own, covering his morning's work. Before he had finished his stomach began to hint to him that lunch would be a good idea, but he went on until, with a sigh of relief, he rolled the report and its duplicates off the typewriter platen. He was stapling the sheets when Mallin came in. Lee looked up.

'Had a useful morning, sir?'

'I'd have done better staying in bed, Bonny. What about you?'

'My report's here, sir.'

Mallin glanced through the top copy. 'Neither nowt nor summat, as they say in these parts, eh? Let's hope you get something out of Trent this afternoon. Had lunch? No? Let's get at it, then.'

Over his tomato soup, Mallin said, 'The Chief tried to put the needle into Mr Trott

97

and me over cracking this Dawson case. In his usual nice way, of course. But how the hell he expects–' He banged his spoon into his plate. 'Fish and chips for me today.'

Lee decided upon the same fare and as he ate Mallin seemed to become happier with life in general. 'There was one odd bit came out this morning,' he said, spearing a chip. 'Keep it to yourself, though, Bonny, because it's highly confidential. An enquiry from Manchester re our friend Louis Pelling. Seems a snout dropped a whisper to one of their chaps that a man of that name was the big shot behind that series of art robberies they've had in Lancashire. Just the name, no more. It meant nothing to them until one of their DS's who was transferred there from Benfield South East remembered our Pelling.'

'And do we have to do a follow-up, sir?'

'No, praise be. The Chief's giving his permission for Manchester to send over two of their officers who've been working on those cases. Thing is, we've to watch we don't alert Pelling in any way. Not that we'd do so, we've nothing to alert him about, more's the pity.'

'You don't like him, I know, sir.'

'I don't like his type. Smart, slick operator,

muscles in here, makes a lot of money fast – and keeps his nose clean. Bonny, there's just got to be something crooked in a chap like that!'

'Illogical, sir, if I may say so. But possibly true.

'You bet your pension it's true! And one of these days – Damn it all to hell, why do fish have so many bones?' He spat an inelegant mouthful on to the side of his plate.

They were drinking their coffee when Lee brought up the subject which had been pestering him at intervals all morning.

'That chap Venner at the university, sir. You saw the comments I made on him in my report. How dangerous can a man like that be, d'you think?'

Mallin considered. 'Depends what material he's got to work on. And whether he means all he spouts or is just trying to be popular, trendy. And you've got to remember the average protesting, down-with-the-pigs student'll be all for law and order time he or she's twenty-five. They'll look back at such as Venner as a daft old clout and wonder why the university paid him a salary at all.'

'He is one of our Dawson contacts, though.'

'And so you want to do a bit of ferreting,

eh? I ought to say no, because its likely to be a sheer waste of your time, boy. But we're stuck on the Dawson case. Also, I like to keep my chaps happy. I'm not telling you to ferret, on the other hand, I'm not forbidding you to.'

'In my own time, of course, sir.'

'And the best of British luck. The same goes for when you see that bloke Trent this afternoon.'

At two-thirty, when he arrived at the High Swing, Lee saw no loungers on the steps, and the vestibule was empty, though the same muted noises came from beyond it. Maybe this was too early for many afternoon clients. Lee struck a bell on the foyer desk.

Raymond Trent appeared in the doorway of his office and his swarthy face seemed to become even darker when he saw who his visitor was.

'I told you all I could about Dawson yesterday, Sergeant. I really can't help you any more. And I'm a busy man.'

'I'm not here about Dawson now, Mr Trent. Have you had any word today from your – waiter, isn't he? – Terry Kershaw?'

Still standing in the doorway, Trent shook his head.

'It isn't his time to clock on yet. He'll be

along later, if you want to see him.'

'I've already seen him, sir. In hospital. He was attacked, on leaving here last night, in the alleyway yonder.'

He jerked a thumb and as he did so he caught a blurred, dodging movement, the glimpse of a half-seen face, in the office behind Trent. The manager closed the door behind him and came forward to the desk.

'Hell, I'm sorry to hear that. It means I'll be short-handed tonight.' He added quickly, 'I hope he's not badly hurt?'

'His condition isn't serious. I'm here to find out, if I can, who set on him, and why?'

Trent shrugged his heavy shoulders. 'There I can't help you. This is the first I've heard of it.'

'Had he got across with any of your customers, do you know? Had a row with one of the lads, say, or tried to make somebody's girl?'

'That slob? He hasn't got the guts for such as that. And let me tell you, Sergeant, we just don't have rows in here. First sign of any, and the trouble-maker is out. For keeps.'

'And who's your bouncer, Mr Trent?'

Trent tapped his own chest. 'Me. I don't need any help, either, no matter how big or rough they come.'

'Cheaper than hiring one. What time did Kershaw leave here last night?'

'Dead on eleven, as usual. We've a rule, last orders by ten forty-five. That gave him a chance to wash up, if you could call it that, the way he did it. More like a break up, it usually is. Anyway, I was going to give him his cards, come Saturday night. I've had enough of his slacking and carelessness.'

'What time did you leave here last night?'

'Let's see... To be exact, twenty past eleven. I had some accounts to do in my office.'

'So you saw nothing of the affair in the alley?'

'I've just told you, haven't I?'

'So you have. And the trouble is, Kershaw himself can't help us much, it seems. But we get that sort of thing frequently. A person's attacked from behind, he goes down and often doesn't see his attackers.' He was watching Trent's small eyes carefully and he thought he saw a momentary spark of relief there. Or was it because he was hoping to note such a spark? 'Thanks for giving me your time, anyway,' he went on. 'I'll have a report to make, but as far as I can see, that'll be the end of it.'

He turned and left the building, noting that the entrance and the steps were still clear of hangers-about. He had a shrewd idea that, on the previous day, when Terry Kershaw had caught him up and spoken to him, their meeting then had been observed. And reported, probably to Trent. So he walked on some fifty yards, then turned suddenly and retraced his steps. This time he went across the vestibule, round the end of the reception desk, and tapped on the door of Trent's office.

Trent's voice called, 'Who is it?' and Lee at once opened the door and stepped into the office.

It was a small, square room with a table in the centre, at which Trent was sitting, facing another man, a big, heavily-built fellow with a broad, deeply-jowled face and a small, thin-lipped mouth. He stared at Lee, then turned his head away as Trent sprang up from his chair, his flattened features suffused with rage.

'What the hell d'you think you're doing, copper? walking in like this? I – I–' His anger almost choked him.

'I knocked,' Lee said blandly, 'and you said "Come in," didn't you?'

'I said nothing of the sort, and you damn

well know it!'

'Sorry.' Lee smiled gently at him and then turned to the other man. 'And how are you, Sammy? Did you have a nice time in Walton?'

He was promptly told to get stuffed. Samuel Gale, inevitably known to his friends as Windy, had just been released after serving three years for committing grievous bodily harm with intent to rob. It wasn't his first GBH conviction, either.

Lee shook his head in mock disapproval. 'You shouldn't take that attitude you know, Sammy. A spell in jail is supposed to be rehabilitating. 'You're expected to come out a wiser and a better man.'

Trent broke in with a shout. 'Cut it out, can't you? I asked you why you busted in here.'

'I'm only doing my duty, Mr Trent.' Lee's tones were still placid. 'I omitted to ask you just now if anything unusual happened here last night which could possibly have a bearing on the assault on Terence Kershaw.'

'I caught the young bastard snooping–' Trent's anger had made him incautious for a moment but he pulled himself up quickly. 'Yeah, snooping around the cash desk. I knew he was short of bread and it looked to me as if he was making a play for a quick dip. That's another reason why I'm sacking him.'

'Thanks again for your help. I'm sorry I had to interrupt you. Good afternoon, gentlemen.'

He retreated in good style, ignoring the words which were flung after him. He wasn't at all displeased with himself. He'd proved his suspicion that it was Windy Gale whom he had glimpsed in Trent's office. That two such men as Gale and Trent should be in conference was something quite worth mulling over.

Back at HQ he rang St Aidan's Hospital and was told Terence Kershaw had been sent home that afternoon. Lee was certain he'd do no good by visiting the Kershaws' house again. Terry had determined not to talk, it was unlikely any pressure from Lee would make him change his mind.

Lee spent the rest of the afternoon on routine jobs in the CID office, knocked off at five o'clock, went along to the police gym for his usual Thursday evening workout, then home to cook and eat an evening meal. It was almost eight o'clock when he went down to his car again. He had noted Dr Venner's address from the directory, and it hadn't surprised him to find that Venner, like William Holder and the Nortons, lived in the Northfield district. It was one which was highly popular with teachers, university staff and other professional people.

Ellerby Close, Venner's address, proved to be a quiet, secluded street, end-stopped at the top of its slope. Venner's house was on the corner round which Lee drove into the Close, a large villa with a lawn in front and flower borders running along each side of it. Lee frowned in annoyance. Keeping observation on that house was going to be awkward, especially as a car was parked outside the semi-detached villa opposite. He had hoped to park his own car in that spot.

He drove to the top of the Close and found a turning circle there. As he came down the street again, a car swung in past Venner's house, a one-man Panda patrol car. Lee pulled into the kerb and halted there, cutting out his engine. The Panda drew up opposite the house, Number 3, directly beyond the parked car Lee had noticed. The patrolman got out of the Panda, went up the drive of Number 3, looked at the windows, tried the front door and walked round to the back. He returned in a matter of seconds, slid into the Panda, reversed out of the Close and drove off.

Lee started his own car again and this time he drove out of the Close to the cross road which led into it. He noted that Numbers 1 and 3 each had deep porches before their front doors. There were lights in Number 1 and also in Venner's house opposite. Lee left his car on the wider road outside the Close and walked back.

The front door of Venner's house opened as he passed it and the figure of a woman was silhouetted in the hall light. Lee's quick glance showed him a dumpy figure in some sort of flowing, loose dress. Long, stringy hair cascaded down each side of her face and the street lamp glinted on the spectacles she wore. She called, 'Puss! Puss!' and a cat came running from a corner of the lawn and halted, tail upraised, to rub itself against the woman's legs. Then the door was closed again.

Lee went up the drive of Number 3 and ensconsed himself in one of the inner corners of the porch. He had a distinct feeling he was wasting his time. If Venner were at home, he and his wife were now settling down for the rest of the evening. Was he himself likely to learn any more than that Venner had a wife – assuming that was who the woman was – a cat and the grey Volkswagon he could see under the car port at the side of the house?

He couldn't – or, rather, he preferred not to – go snooping up the drive and listening at the house windows, though there was one big bay, very inviting-looking, which faced the road. There were few people about but he wasn't prepared to be caught acting suspiciously. If he had had anything definite on Venner, well, that would be different. He decided to wait for exactly half an hour, no longer.

After a while he began to feel chilly, there was frost in the air tonight. The colder he became, the more his enthusiasm was nipped. He began to think of his cosy flat, a light supper, a long drink and an early night for once.

He knew how time could drag when a man was 'on obbo,' but he was surprised, when he raised the luminous dial of his watch to his eyes, that he had been in that porch only a bare quarter of an hour. So he'd give it another five minutes and pack it in, going home and ignoring the hunch which had brought him here.

Those hunches – all experienced CID men knew of them. You set out on an uncharted line, for no reason you could put into words, solely because in some inner way you were directed. And there was a compulsion to follow that line which you couldn't avoid.

He was about to step out of the porch when a dark green Mini-Cooper, showing signs of age, swung round the corner and pulled up at Venner's house. Lee halted his own movement. Two men got out of the car and went up the drive. Lee recognized the hulking form, the huge round head, of Windy Gale, whom he had seen that afternoon in Trent's office. The other man was smaller, slimmer, slightly bow-legged. There was something familiar about him but Lee couldn't place him there and then. The CID man drew back into concealment. It looked as if there was something doing here after all.

Venner answered the door to his visitors. He seemed to be expecting them. He ushered them into the hall, nodding in friendly fashion to Windy and shaking hands with the other man as if he were meeting him for the first time. Then the door was closed. Lee looked up at one of the front bedroom windows where a light had just been put on. The woman he had seen came to the window and drew the curtains. The light behind them remained on as he stood watching. He guessed the woman had either been sent to bed, or had gone there voluntarily, as soon as the visitors arrived. She had not, it seemed, been wanted to help entertain the two men.

Tempted as he was to move up to that front window and try his luck at a spot of eavesdropping, Lee resisted it. It just wasn't safe.

He left his shelter and went to his car. He drove it in to Ellerby Close again and parked it near the top of the street, facing towards Venner's house. Then he settled down to wait in it.

Forty minutes later the two men left Venner's, their host seeing them off from the front door. Lee started his car engine, and, as the two reached the gates, he switched his headlights full on. The men turned, caught in the sudden beam. Of course! Chalky White, whose given name was Edwin, that was who the small man was. A petty crook, always trying to get into the big-time stuff, and never making it.

Lee switched off his headlights at once and drove forward on his sidelights only. He passed the Mini-Cooper as the two were settling themselves into it. They didn't even glance in his direction. He drove home, satisfied that his hunch, once again, hadn't played him false.

Chapter Seven

Superintendent Trott shook his head doubt-fully. 'I don't like the idea of anybody, university professor or whoever, entertaining such as Gale and White. But Venner told you he went to that High Swing place to do a bit of research on the types who use it, Lee. It could be that he's studying the criminal character, too. And,' he added, 'I can't see how all this is helping us with the Dawson case.'

They were seated alone in the super's office, Mallin having a Court job to attend to that Friday morning.

'We've no direct evidence to connect Venner with Dawson, I admit, sir. But I'm convinced Venner's ideas are dangerous, fanatical. I know it sounds a trifle wild, but suppose he were planning some sort of – well, coup, and had called in such as White and Gale to help him?'

Trott frowned. 'Let's keep our feet on the ground, Sergeant. Let's not get into the airy-fairy regions. Our job is to crack a case, and we're stuck with it at the moment.' One of his desk telephones rang and he picked it up irritably. 'Yes?... Who?... Right, show him in.'

He recradled the instrument and blew out his cheeks. 'Here's one for the Top Ten! Louis Pelling craving an interview!'

'Angels and ministers of grace defend us!' Lee got up quickly, but Trott flung out a hand.

'Stay where you are, lad. I'll need somebody to hold my hand, or before I know where I am I'll be accusing that flamer of every unsolved crime on the books.'

The door opened and a cadet constable said, 'Mr Pelling, sir,' before he retired. Without haste, Lee rose and brought an extra chair to his super's desk. He knew Trott wouldn't want any sort of welcoming fuss shown to the man he suspected of being behind around dozen of jobs in Benfield.

Louis Pelling was tall, wide-shouldered, with thick lips and a heavily-beaked nose. Black hair, threaded with white, was thick and recently permed. He wore a tan shirt and matching tie, his sharply-tailored suit was russet, his shoes round-toed suede. He was clean shaven with an old-fashioned short-back-and-sides hair style. His hands beyond the plain gold cuff links of his shirt sleeves were big, powerful, the backs dark with a thick growth of hair. Each of his middle fingers carried a heavy ring, one in amethyst and gold, the other with a sparkling ruby.

He hitched up his trousers, sat down and nodded to Trott.

'Good morning, Superintendent.' His voice was resonant, his accent carefully controlled. 'I thought it was high time I had a little chat with you.'

His tone was that of the headmaster who has summoned a small boy to his study because the little wretch has been slacking. Lee saw Trott's mouth tighten.

'We're rather too busy, sir, to indulge in chats. If you are here on business, please state it.'

It was an opening which was only just within the bounds of courtesy, but Pelling shrugged it off. He turned his head slowly towards Lee.

'I don't think we've met, have we? If you are staying – well, I like to know who I'm talking to.'

'Detective Sergeant Lee,' Trott replied. 'One of my mot experienced officers.'

Pelling nodded pleasantly. 'Nice to know

you, Sergeant. And I believe it's because of you that I'm here today. Trent, my manager at the Carlton Street place, tells me you've been around two days in succession, questioning him.'

'On my instructions, sir.' Trott was hardly bothering to conceal his antagonism. Lee judged it was time he gave the super a chance to cool down.

'On the first occasion, sir, it was because of the killing of Wilfred Dawson, which we are investigating. Dawson's landlady had stated that her lodger frequented the High Swing. We were finding it difficult to learn much about Dawson's background, so we've interviewed all the people we can who knew him. Mr Trent was most helpful though he couldn't assist us much, as it happened.'

'Surely, Mr Pelling' – Trott's voice was more level now – 'you haven't come here to complain that your manager was inter-viewed?'

Pelling threw back his head and laughed. 'Good Lord, no, Superintendent! I only wish he could have helped you more. But the thing is, here I own a discotheque and dance hall, one of the frequenters of which – though Trent tells me he was by no means a regular – gets himself killed. This, in my

114

book, smears the image of the place somewhat.'

'Because you suspect someone who also frequented it was Dawson's killer?'

The carefully-tended head was shaken. 'I don't, otherwise you'd have heard all about it by now. From me. No, I run my properties cleanly, all above board, as you people know. And I aim to keep that policy intact.' He drew his chair closer to Trott's desk. 'If you've any evidence, or suspicions, Superintendent, that any of my High Swing clients were involved in this man's death, I beg of you tell me who they are. I'll see they won't cause any more trouble of any sort at the High Swing.'

Trott frowned again, in genuine puzzlement now.

'Surely, Mr Pelling, you can't be so naïve to expect we'd give information like that away, to a member of the general public, even if we had it?'

Pelling nodded and leaned back. 'Of course not. Stupid of me to mention it, of course. Got a little carried away, I suppose. But I'm rather proud of the High Swing's reputation, you know. Such places are often trouble centres – which is no news to you, I realize.'

'You mentioned you'd been told Sergeant Lee visited that place again yesterday. Any complaints about that, sir?'

'Ah!' Pelling sat forward again. 'Yes. No question of complaint, but I did learn that one of my employees there had been beaten up in the adjoining alley after he had left work. Trent assures me he knows nothing about it, that he first heard of it from Sergeant Lee. It seems the youth concerned – Kershaw – was inefficient and due for dismissal. But that doesn't alter the fact that he was one of my employees. Trent had omitted, very carelessly, in my opinion, to find out how the boy was, what damage he had received. I'm here to ask for this information from you. So that if there's anything I can do... Who was it set on him?'

'He either doesn't know or he won't tell,' Lee answered.

'Trent will have his address,' Trott pointed out. He knew that same address was in Lee's possession but he'd go to hell if he made things easy for his bête noir in even the smallest way. 'Kershaw is out of hospital now. You'll be able to see him at his home.'

Pelling looked at the expensive gold watch on his left wrist. 'Yes, I must do that. Can't fit it in this morning, though.' He sprang to

116

his feet, lithely, like an athlete in full training. 'I'm a busy man, and so are you, Mr Trott, as you took care to remind me just now. But I feel this talk has cleared the air, for me, at any rate. I'm relieved to find that image of the High Swing still untarnished in the official mind.'

He nodded to them both, gave them a good morning to share between them, and was out of the office before Lee could get up and open the door for him.

Trott watched him go. Then he turned his face, now set in its normal lines of gloom, to Lee.

'And what was all that in aid of, d'you think?'

'Sounding us out, sir? Working the old pump handle?'

'Possibly. Maybe I cracked down on him too sharply when he began to ask questions. If we'd played him on a bit, he might have let something out... Though he's not that type, I suppose. Too cagey altogether.'

'You've known him longer, and you know him better than I, sir. Would you rate him as a possible suspect in the Dawson case?'

'If you mean, did he put a bullet in Dawson's brain, the answer is no, very definitely. If it was a case of getting somebody else to do it, again I'd say no. I've studied this man, Lee. I know – without definite proof to hang on him – that he's been behind half a dozen or more steals. Those art thefts, the wage snatches – you know the tally as well as I do. But he won't employ gunmen. He has an absolute dread of guns. To me, that's his only virtue. No, if for some reason he wanted to put Dawson out of the way, it would have been by another method.'

'I'd have liked to have asked him if he knew Venner, sir.'

'He wouldn't have told you if he does, if it didn't suit him to. And, as I've warned you before, don't get Venner on the brain too much.' He turned as a knock sounded on the office door. 'Come in!'

It was the cadet who had brought Pelling to them.

'Excuse me, sir, but there are two people at the desk wanting to speak to Sergeant Lee. Brother and sister, name of Kershaw.'

The CID men exchanged glances. Trott said, 'You'd better see them in here. I've got to go out, anyway, and from what you told me about this lad, talking to a stranger – myself – could put him off.'

'Very good, sir,' Lee answered, and the cadet, a keen type, sprang across to the stand in the corner to lift down Trott's hat and coat. 'You can show them in,' Lee said when the Superintendent had gone.

He moved into the chair behind the desk when he had placed the other two chairs to face him.

Marion Kershaw came in quickly, her auburn hair and bright smile seeming to bring sunshine with her. Her brother was more laggard, it was clear he wished himself anywhere than in a CID office. His bruises were fading, though he moved a little stiffly, from his still-strapped ribs, Lee guessed.

He welcomed his visitors, saw them settled into the chairs. He sat down again behind the desk.

'Well,' he asked pleasantly, 'and why this honour?'

Marion answered at once. 'Terry didn't want to come, but I persuaded him, Mr Lee.'

'She ordered me to,' Terry said sulkily. 'Just because she's a few years older, she's bossed me around ever since I was a kid.'

'Elder sisters are like that,' Lee returned. 'I should know – I have one. Anyway, you're here. So what?'

Marion nodded to her brother. 'Your scene, love.'

He wriggled uncomfortably. 'It's all very well for you. But they told me if I squealed to the cops about what they'd done, I'd get worse next time.'

'Who said what?' Lee asked patiently.

'Ralph Jowett and his mob, when they'd done me over.'

'Ah, yes. We know Master Jowett. Probation, Detention Centre, Approved School. Does he and what you say is his mob use the High Swing, then? I understood, both from Mr Trent and Mr Pelling, the owner, that such types as Jowett were not allowed there.'

'Pelling doesn't know everything that goes on,' Terry muttered. 'As long as there's no trouble...'

'Why were you done over, then?'

'One of the cats saw me talking to you – you know, when you left the Swing and I come after you. He told Ray Trent.'

'And Trent asked you what we'd talked about?'

'Yes. I thought quick and told him I'd recognized you as being one of the detectives as works from this place. I guessed, I said, you'd come to the Swing for information about something and maybe I could help you becos I see what's going on in there more'n Ray Trent does, him often being in his office.'

'Do you think Trent believed you?'

'I dunno. He stared at me for a bit and then he said it would be best for me to mind me own business.'

'But, surely, you didn't get that beating-up later on just because you'd spoken to me?'

Terry licked his lips. 'I don't reckon so. See, I promised you, didn't I, I'd try and find out what went on in Ray's office, getting an earful through that hatch I told you about. I thought, when Mr Pelling rolled up as usual, they might talk about this Dawson as was shot. Remember?' Lee nodded. 'Well, I managed to get the hatch open a bit and there was somebody in there talking to Ray. But it wasn't Mr Pelling. This cat had a sort of lah-di-dah voice, used a lot of long words. Ray kept calling him Jim, like he was saying Ray all the time. So I think to meself they must be good pals.'

'You heard what they were saying?'

'I heard bits. This Jim said something about it was a big mistake to go as far as that and now things had got dangerous. And Ray said to stop worrying, everything would be okay. Then this Jim said something like, "Well, he's paid for it, but in future I'll give the orders, remember." Just at that I heard

121

the office door open and Ralph Jowett speak. He says, "Mr Pelling's car's just pulling up, Ray," and Ray says, "Right. You scarper quick," but I think that was to this Jim and not to Jowett. There's a back way out of Ray's office, you see. All went quiet for a little bit, and then I heard Ray say, "Ah, good evening sir." And I didn't hear no more because I had some orders to fill at the counter and when I got a chance to listen again, all was quiet. Then Ray came into the dance hall and stopped there for a while so I reckoned Mr Pelling had gone. I managed to close the hatch when nobody was watching, and that's all I know.'

His sullen tone had been maintained throughout his recital, now he looked at his sister as if to say, 'Well, I've done what you said I had to, so let's get out of here.'

But Lee hadn't finished with him. 'Were there any of Jowett's mob in the hall while you were trying to listen?'

'Coulda bin one or two of 'em. I didn't only notice one, bloke called Baker.'

'Who might have seen you standing by the hatch, probably leaning towards it. So the lesson you were given in the alley was to teach you not to do that sort of thing again and that if you had heard anything you shouldn't, you'd better not bring it to us here.'

Terry grunted. 'I've had enough of that place, anyway. I'm packing in working there.'

'You're getting the sack at the end of this week,' Lee said. 'Trent told me as much. But I'm glad you came along here, Terry. I think you've been helpful.'

'It was our Marion as made me. If we've bin seen coming to this place and I get done again, it'll be her fault.'

'You're talking nonsense, Terry,' Marion said briskly. 'Who on earth could have seen us? We came straight from home,' she told Lee. 'We got on the bus just outside our house. It stops at the Universal stores, we went in at one end and came out at the other hardly twenty yards from here.'

'If you're at all worried,' Lee said, 'you can leave by the back entrance here. There's a passage which leads out to Broadgate.'

'Good,' Marion said. She got up. 'Come along, Terry.' Lee went to the door and opened it for them. She looked up at him.

'I've been wondering Mr Lee. This man Jim who talked in an educated voice and who was at the High Swing. I know some-one who fits those three categories – name, accent and place frequented.'

'So do I, Marion. Dr Venner. But didn't you know a copper's boots are always soled heavily with lead? That's to stop him from jumping to conclusions.'

He gave her a wink and a smile, saw the pair of them into the charge of a police-woman who would guide them out by the rear premises and was looking over the notes he had made when Inspector Mallin walked in. He sniffed loudly.

'What you doing in here, Bonny? Got a quick promotion?'

Lee told him all. Mallin shrugged off his coat and flung it over a chair. He hitched himself up on the edge of the desk.

'Been quite a social morning, it seems, while I've been wasting my own time.'

'You can't mean Joe Lacy got off, sir?'

'He only got sent down for five, and I was hoping for at least seven. So Louis Pelling arrives here, all sweetness and light, and the Kershaw kid comes clean. Anything else?'

Lee told his chief of his own spell of observation the previous evening and what had come of it.

Mallin frowned. 'I don't like the sound of that. It hasn't necessarily anything to do with the Dawson job, but wherever Windy

Gale goes, there you can expect trouble. And where does he and White come into all this?'

'That puzzles me too, sir. But if there was skulduggery being discussed in that High Swing office, it seems Pelling wasn't in on it. Everything broke up when he appeared.'

Mallin fingered his chin. 'Let's face it, the only unexplained contact with Dawson up to now is this one with Trent. And, possibly, with Venner. But we can't put either of them on the grill. No evidence. I wonder if we could get anything out of White?'

Lee glanced at his watch. 'If he's still running true to form, he'll be in the Rose of York at this moment, dallying with a pint. Suppose we send somebody along to chat him up in a general way?'

'I'll leave it to you.' Mallin picked up his coat and turned to go into his own room. Lee walked along to the general CID office, where he found Detective Constable Aston doing a one-finger act on a typewriter. He looked up.

'Hi, sarge! We've got that chemist's break-in sewn up. Manny Belton, without a doubt. He was careless with his dabs – these junkies often are – and we've two positive identifications from reliable witnesses. Ivor Jones has gone to pick him up.'

'Good. You can leave what you're doing, Dave. I want you to nip along to the Rose of York…'

And so it came about, some ten minutes later, that Edwin White, seated quietly in a corner with the bottom half of his second pint before him, looked up to see Aston standing with a glass of cider in his hand.

'Mind if I join you, Chalky?'

White scowled. 'Can't stop yer, can I? You ain't welcome, though. I'll tell yer that much.'

'Now, there's no need to be like that.' Aston sat down opposite. 'Not when I've come to tell you something you ought to know.'

'And what the bleeding 'ell might that be?'

Aston took a swallow of his drink. 'Last night an old lady was knocked down, had her bag snatched. Near St Giles's Church. But when we got a whisper you were responsible, Mr Lee wouldn't have it. "No, not Chalky," he said. "He might pinch a rattle off a baby, but he wouldn't lay a finger on the kid to do so. Chalky doesn't go in for violence."'

'I should damn well think not, mate! Whoever told you that lie?' He emptied his

126

glass in an almost virtuous manner.

'So it was just a case of Liz trying to get you into trouble again, eh?'

'Oh, that bitch, was it?' Liz Maguire – she had reverted to her maiden name – had broken with Chalky after the biggest, most thunderous row conceivable. Witnesses claimed it should be in the Guinness Book of Records. And time had not closed the breach. The reverse, rather. Liz was determined to get her own back, any way she could.

'Look, Mr Aston.' Anger at his former wife swept away all Chalky's caution. 'I can prove she's a liar. I was out last night at a place Northfield way, with a pal. Me pal had done a bit of business for a feller as lives there, and he went to collect. Took me along with him becos this feller might want another job done, see, and I might be able to help. All legit, of course,' he added hurriedly.

'Fair enough. That'll do for me.' Aston finished his drink, picked up Chalky's glass and took it to the bar for a refill.'

Chapter Eight

At two o'clock that Friday afternoon Marion Kershaw left the huge concrete-and-glass building which was known as the Arts Block at Benfield University and crossed the campus to the Department of Sociology. She used the lift and found the departmental secretary just back from her lunch break.

'I'm Marion Kershaw,' she told the secretary. 'Arts Department. Could I make an appointment to see Dr Venner, do you think? It's a private matter but I won't take up much of his time.'

The secretary looked at the girl's neatly-dressed hair, her spotless apple-green two-piece, her immaculate shoes. Hardly the type, she would have thought, to want a private interview with James Venner. But she smiled encouragingly.

'He's lecturing at three this afternoon,' she said. 'He hasn't any engagements before then as far as I know. He promised he'd go through a pile of essays which are overdue for return, when he came back from lunch.

Whenever that will be.'

'Woman, the time is now!' Venner's deep voice sounded from the doorway. 'And who is this beautiful flower, so conventional-seeming, such a product of an outworn system? Don't you realize, child, that that gear you are wearing epitomises your slavery to the rotten ideals of an age long past?'

Marion looked at the tubby figure with its fuzzy-wuzzy hair, its scraggy beard, its hippy clothing. She felt, though it was an un-ladylike thought, that like Roger Ineson, she wanted to spit. Instead, she said pleasantly, 'I happen to like my chains, sir. I may be wrong there, but, you know, we haven't all seen the light yet.'

'Miss Marion Kershaw, Arts Department,' the secretary broke in primly. 'Could you spare her a few moments?'

'I can spare her almost an hour. With delight. Follow Jim into his sanctum, Marion Kershaw, and there we will discourse.'

'There are those essays–' the secretary began. She was promptly told to get stuffed. Venner closed the door of his room, sat down behind his desk.

'There's a chair in the corner there,' he said. 'Bring it across, eh? Now then, how can I help you?'

Marion folded her hands in her lap. 'Dr Venner, you must be aware that your views, your opinions, are known and quoted all through this university.'

He laughed. 'They should be. I sow the good seed wherever and whenever I can. And my friends call me Jim, Marion.'

She managed to giggle coyly. 'It doesn't seem right, somehow... But, anyway – er – Jim, I pride myself on my straightforwardness.'

'So you should. It's your right to say what you think, without considering other people's feelings. It's the only path to self-liberation. So you're going to ask me a personal question. I know it. I can read most people's minds. So...?'

'It's just this, and you must forgive me if I sound impertinent. These theories you preach – do you really believe in them, or could they be – well, just a sort of gimmick?'

'I'm glad you asked that. I think we're going to be friends and I don't want you to have any false impressions of me.' He sat forward. 'I believe in them absolutely. I am convinced we shall never change this present filthy social system, based on authority, outworn beliefs and a stupid code of laws, until we smash the whole lot up, pulverize them, get rid of them for good.'

His voice had risen, his amber-brown eyes were alight. Then the buzzer on his desk sounded. His shoulders drooped, he sighed as he put out a thick finger, with grime-rimmed nails, to press a key.

'Look, love, whatever it is, just leave it, will you? I can't be interrupted now. If it's somebody to see me, just tell them to go to bloody hell, will you?'

The Secretary's voice came clearly to Marion. 'I can't do that. It's the Bursar on the line. He wants to speak to you personally.'

'Oh, well … Okay, let's have him.' He picked up a telephone and shrugged at Marion.

'Sorry about that,' he said two minutes later, after a conversation which had consisted, on his part, mostly of grunts. 'But you know what these old goats in authority are. They're not going to last long, though. No, Marion, the Big Day is very near. The organization of student power to the full – that's all we need and we're going to get it. Oh, there are laggards yet, but in time – soon we'll gather them in.' The fire had come back to his eyes. 'Then, with fitting leadership, with the right, the only, man at the top – by thunder, girl, we'll remake the world!'

His broad chest was rising and falling rapidly. He forced a grin to his lips and she saw the effort he made to relax.

'It sounds marvellous,' she said, but she put doubt into her voice. 'If it could be done. One thinks of others who sought world power – the Caesars, Napoleon, Hitler...'

'But surely, the only value of history to man is to show him the mistakes of the past in order that he may avoid them?'

'True enough, Jim, but I'm still not completely convinced you're right. Much as I'd like to ... to be surer.'

And then the buzzer sounded again. Venner stared at it, clearly willing himself to take no notice of it. But his finger went out to the key.

'Professor Dover is here, Dr Venner,' Marion heard. 'You asked him to come and see you when you met in the Senior Common Room after lunch today. I'll show him in, of course.'

Her final sentence wasn't a question, it was a statement of firm fact. Venner didn't answer. He released the key and turned again to Marion.

'No use, no use at all. They won't leave me alone.' His voice was peevish now. 'Never enough time to get on with my real job in life!'

'Maybe we could talk again, when you're less busy?'

'And that's not likely to happen at this foul place. Look, tell you what, Marion. How about coming along to my home one evening, where we can really talk. My wife, I know, would be delighted to see you.'

Marion looked doubtful. 'My evenings are rather full. I live at home, you see, and there are certain duties to be carried out there. In fact, this evening is the only one I have free for almost a week.'

'But that would be fine! Any time from seven-thirty onwards.' He glanced up as the secretary brought a tall West Indian into the room and Marion rose hastily. 'Be with you in a trice, Paul,' Venner said, scribbling on a pad in front of him. He tore off a sheet and handed it to Marion. 'That's the address. 'Voir, then.'

She walked down the stairs and made her way to the Union building. In one of the reading rooms. Roger Ineson put down a textbook on agricultural economy and rose, stretching his long limbs.

'Well, my sweet, any luck?'

'He took the bait like a lamb, if I may mix metaphors. He sees me as his latest disciple and I've promised to go to his house tonight, for more of the dope, I suppose.'

Roger frowned. 'You'll do nothing of the sort! I'm not having you indulging in cosy chats with crazy profs in their domestic dens.'

'Have no fears, mate. His wife will be present. And you'll run me out there, won't you?'

'Sure. But what did you make of him? Just a windbag, eh?'

'I can't make up my mind about him, though he does give me the impression of being – well, devoted. Like a sort of militant zealot who's waiting for the right moment to strike. But I'll be clearer on that when we've had our little talk tonight.'

'You're sure it's wise, Marion, going on with this?'

'Look, love. Somebody beat up my kid brother. I'm sure it was because he was trying to listen-in to Trent and the man who was with Trent. I'm also sure that man was Venner. I told Sergeant Lee as much – and got the brush-off.'

'Which you might have expected. And I don't imagine you'll get anything from Venner tonight bar another long ranting sermon. Talk about a sheer waste of an evening!'

134

Detective Constable David Aston was engaged to a girl who worked in the Benfield City Council offices and he had been hoping that Friday evening to spend some time with her. But Bonny Lee had ruled differently. With Inspector Mallin's approval, Aston had been ordered to spend the two hours from seven o'clock until nine that evening standing in a draughty porch while he watched the house of a university professor where nothing at all was likely to happen during those two hours.

He had left his car a couple of streets away and had slipped through the gate and up the drive to the porch of the untenanted house at a moment when Ellerby Close was completely empty of people. He knew he wouldn't be flushed by any patrolman tonight; the local station had been warned about that. He propped himself up in the least windy corner of the porch and settled down with his customary patience.

Nothing out of the ordinary took place for twenty minutes. Then a lank-haired youth in a belted raincoat came round the corner into the Close, stood there to light a cigarette and then walked slowly up the Close, on the opposite side from Aston. He turned his head and stared at Venner's house as he

135

passed it, then went on out of Aston's sight – he probably lived in one of the houses higher up, the detective surmised. But within a couple of minutes he walked past again, still on the far side of the road. He regained the corner, and beckoned. Three other youths joined him at once. Venner's drive gates stood open and the four, without hesitation, walked up the drive. But before they reached the house they split up, two of them passing round one side of it, two disappearing round the other.

Aston was puzzled. If they were legitimate visitors to Venner's house, and had been told to go to the back door, why hadn't they gone there in a bunch? Why split up like that? Was a spot of burglary on the cards, then? Break in at the back while the Venners were watching television in one of the front rooms? There was certainly a light showing behind the curtains of the bay window which faced the road. But, unless the idea was a full-scale attack on the inhabitants, laying them out before looting the place, the method was all wrong. They should have left one man, at least, to watch out in front of the house.

Aston took a couple of steps outside the porch and listened. It wasn't easy, for cars were continually passing along the main road off which the Close led. But he couldn't hear any sounds of violence, no breaking glass nor splintering wood. And his orders had been only to watch Venner's house, to report any unusual happenings and visitors there. He'd keep on the alert, though, he promised himself, and at the first sounds of villainy he'd be across the road and up Venner's drive like a rocket.

At that moment a young woman came briskly into Ellerby Close. As she passed beneath the lamp which lit the corner, Aston saw she had a trim figure and a face which was worth a second look, even from an engaged man. She paused at Venner's gates, clearly checking the number painted on one of the posts, then she also went up the drive. But her objective was the front door, she mounted the steps and pressed the illuminated bell-stud. Almost at once the door opened and a short, tubby man clad in what looked like an overall made welcoming motions at her, ushered her in, closed the door.

Well, Aston thought, that visitor seemed to be legitimate enough. And still there appeared to be no funny business going on across the way. He retreated, shivering a little, into the porch, alert for the next happening, if any.

Half an hour went draggingly by. Twice he thought he saw movement in the shadows at one side of the house; he couldn't imagine what the four youth could be doing. Surely, if they had intended a break-in, they'd have been in and out by now? And, surely, they weren't waiting until the household was in bed and asleep? He supposed it was possible the quartet had designs on another house, say one in the adjoining street, which they intended to get at from the back, by way of Venner's property... He was letting his imagination run away with him, the odds were that the four had been invited to the house and had gone round to the back door to be let in there. But then, why had they split up as they had done? And why had the first one reconnoitred the Close before bringing his three pals into it?

An ancient Ford Popular chugged into the Close. As it came, Aston saw its driver, who was young and solidly built, was alone in the car. He drove up to the turnway and came down again on Aston's side. He pulled up almost directly opposite the CID man, partly blocking his view of Venner's house. The car engine was switched off, its driver raised a wrist to peer at his watch and then sat, tapping his fingers impatiently on the steering wheel. Five minutes later, during which time he looked at his watch repeatedly, he flung himself out of the car and went striding across the road and into Venner's drive. But he had taken only a few steps along it when he seemed to change his mind. He turned sharply and came out into the road again, standing there to stare at Venner's house. Aston saw his shoulders rise and fall in a shrug, the watch was consulted again and its owner moved slowly back to his car, leaning against the bonnet and beginning to whistle softly through his teeth.

He straightened up with a jerk when the front door of Venner's house opened and the girl who had gone in over half an hour since appeared, with the tubby, fuzzy-haired man in tow. Aston caught broken sentences – 'Most interesting ... given me a lot to think about...' from the girl, and 'Glad to be helpful ... must come again soon ... another talk...' from the man. He stood watching her walk down the drive, at the gates she turned to wave to him. He went in, shut the door. The girl hurried across the street to the man by the car. He greeted her grumpily.

'Half an hour, you said, and it's nearly

three-quarters. I was just coming in to get you.'

She put a hand on his arm. 'Sorry, love. I left as soon as I could. And his wife was there all the time. She only left us alone a few seconds while she made coffee.'

'Did you get anything out of him?'

'I'll tell you all about it in the car. One thing I am sure of, he's more dangerous than most people think. Look, it was sweet of you to wait. I thought he'd never stop talking, and then his wife reminded him of some television programme they'd planned to see.' She was moving round the car to the passenger's door as she added, 'They asked me to stay and watch it with them, but I said I had to be getting back.'

The young man grunted, slammed himself behind the wheel of the car, shut the door with a bang. The engine roared and the car moved off, out of the Close.

Aston watched its rear lights disappear as he thought over what the girl had said. Obviously, he would be just wasting his time if he continued with his observation job. It was well turned eight and it seemed Venner was expecting no more visitors tonight, since he was settling down in front of the box. But there was still that little puzzle of the four youths. Surely, if they had been admitted to Venner's house by the back door, they were there while the girl had paid her visit, yet she hadn't mentioned others in the house except Venner and his wife.

Aston came out of the porch, crossed the road, went up the drive to Venner's house. He rang the bell and it was only a matter of seconds before the door opened again and he was confronted by the short, stout man.

'Yes?'

'Sorry to disturb you, sir. I am a police officer.' He thrust his warrant card forward. 'Almost an hour ago, four youths walked up your drive and went round to the back of your house, two on each side of it. I considered this was acting in a suspicious manner. They have not reappeared. Are they with you?'

'Four youths, you say? Good God, no. We've had a visitor, but she's just left. Only my wife and myself in the house.'

'With your permission, sir, I'd like to take a look around your rear premises.' Aston produced a heavy torch from a pocket of his overcoat.

'Half a sec, and I'll come with you.' He stepped back, reached out one arm and brought an anorak into view. He struggled

141

into it, shut the front door and joined Aston on the steps.

'I think it would be best if you watched the front of the house, sir,' Aston said. 'If they're still hanging around the back, and I flush them, give me a shout. All right?'

Venner nodded his bushy head and walked down the drive a few paces, facing the house. Aston stepped quietly to one side of it and looked along the narrow path which led to the rear. The street lights gave him a good view of a flower border stretching away into the back garden. Nothing there. He tried the other side, beyond the garage and car port attached to the house. The border here, and the path, were in shadow. He went along the path, round to the back of the house. Here was darkness, he swept his torch beam from left to right. An area of concrete was backed by the low wall of what seemed to be a terraced border, with an extensive lawn, more flower borders and trees beyond. This back garden was enclosed on its three sides by six-feet high interwoven fencing panels – not an easy route by which to reach the houses beyond, as he had thought might have been the youths' objective.

He found some steps, went down them

and began to examine the fencing on that side of the garden. He had not gone far when a confused shouting broke out at the front of the house. He turned and sprinted back along the side path. Venner was sprawling on the edge of the lawn calling out something which Aston didn't catch. And the four youths he had formerly seen were disappearing through the drive gates.

Aston started after them. Venner, struggling to his knees, grasped at Aston's arm, as if for support, as the detective constable was passing him. Cursing silently, Aston tried to shake Venner off, but the man, gasping out something unintelligible, clung on for several precious seconds while he staggered to his feet. By the time Aston got rid of him, the youths were already away round the corner of the Close. Aston followed at speed. He saw the four pile into an Anglia which was standing round the corner, with a fifth man at the wheel and the engine running. It was on the move when Aston was still twenty yards away. It roared off in the direction of town and he wasn't able to read its mud-covered rear number plate.

He cursed again and went back to Venner. The man was steady on his feet now, rubbing one side of his head.

'They rushed me, from the far path yonder. One had a cosh, but it only hit me a glancing blow. I'm all right, no damages.'

'Did you recognize any of them?'

'Not a single one. What was the game, d'you think?'

'I don't know. But it's not likely they'll come back again tonight. You're sure you're okay?'

'Quite sure. And I won't mention the incident to my wife. I don't wish to upset her.'

Aston agreed, wished him goodnight and went to find his car. No use hanging around here any more, of that he was certain. It was a decision he was to regret later.

Chapter Nine

Kathleen Nolan was a thoroughly contented person. She had the best husband a woman could wish for, two sons, both doing well in their respective jobs and three of the loveliest grandchildren you ever saw. She was fit, so was Jack, her husband, and they loved their jobs as caretakers of Ashcroft House, one of the four three-storey luxury flats which made up Belle Vue Mansions.

Louis Pelling owned the Mansions, he lived on the ground floor of Ashcroft House and had had a one-storey annexe built out at the back of it, where the Nolans lived. Jack Nolan doubled as caretaker of Ashcroft House and maintenance man for all the Mansions, his wife's job was to look after the material comforts of Louis Pelling himself.

On this Saturday morning, having seen to their own breakfasts, Mrs Nolan was preparing a tray on which stood a silver coffee-pot, a Crown Derby cup, saucer and plate. No cream jug nor sugar basin, Mr Pelling always took his coffee black. The plate held fingers of golden toast, lusciously buttered.

Jack Nolan looked up from his newspaper. 'United are playing at home today, love, did I tell you? Our Bob's calling for me this afternoon with the car, and we're watching the match together.'

Kathleen gave a little snort of mock annoyance. 'Now he tells me! All right, I'll ring Bob and ask him to bring Susan and Bridget here with him. It's ages since I saw those kids, and Christine'll be glad to have a free afternoon for once.'

Her husband nodded and returned to the sports page. Kathleen picked up the three newspapers which Pelling read, tucked them under one arm, lifted the tray and went along a short passage to a baize-covered swing door which she pushed open with her shoulder. Jack reached out a hand to grope for his teacup without taking his eyes from the printed word. After an interval of fumbling his fingers found the cup handle – and froze on it.

The scream penetrated even the sound-absorbing properties of the baize-covered door.

Then Jack was on his feet, his chair crashing to the tiled floor. He went at a run along the passage and charged the swing door.

It led directly into the long, wide room which, with a dining alcove at one end, occupied the length of the flat with the exception of a small anteroom giving on to the main hall. Two shallow steps down from the alcove was the owner's combined sitting room and study, a richly-furnished place with its deep-pile carpet, its expensive modern furniture, the carefully-chosen pictures on its walls. Wealth spoke, too, in the walnut desk and matching swivel chair, backed by bookcases in light oak, which stood near the outer wall of the room.

Fully dressed, Louis Pelling was sprawled across the desk, his head turned sideways on it, his arms hanging stiffly, his feet twisted beneath the chair. Blood was spattered over his upturned cheek, below a bullet wound in the temple.

Mrs Nolan was standing in the alcove, staring, rigid. She still held the tray in hands stiffened with shock, though the papers had fallen to the floor. Her mouth, from which that one piercing scream had come, was open, her lips frozen in horror. Jack took the tray from her and set it down on a table clatteringly. He seized her shoulders and forced her down into a chair. She gasped, began to pant like a swimmer who has gone

147

too far from shore and is suddenly aware of the fact. Then Jack went forward, stiff-legged, to look more closely at the figure across the desk. He felt his stomach heave as he turned away. But he controlled himself and reached out for the cream-coloured telephone on the desk.

Mallin and Lee were sitting in the kitchen of the caretakers' flat. Beyond, in Pelling's apartments, the photographers and the dabs experts were going stolidly about their work and, among the vehicles crowded in the forecourt of Ashcroft House, an ambulance was waiting.

Mrs Nolan, huddled in a corner, was still shivering spasmodically in spite of the second cup of brandy-laced tea her husband had insisted she should drink. Her teeth chattered on the rim of the cup as she raised it, with a grimace of distaste, to her lips. But reaction was making her husband talk, loudly and almost increasingly. Mallin broke in when he was beginning, for the third time, a detailed account of what he had said and done that morning.

'All right, Mr Nolan. We've got the picture. Mrs Nolan took in Mr Pelling's breakfast tray, saw what had happened, screamed. You dashed in, made sure he was dead and rang us. You didn't touch anything except the telephone and, leaving everything as it was, you brought your wife back here and looked after her. And you are surprised Sergeant Lee and I got here so quickly. But we do work on Saturday mornings, you know, and we'd been at our desks some time when your call came through. Now then, I'm going to ask you quite a lot of questions. Okay?'

'Anything I can do to help, Inspector. Anything at all.'

'Good. Start by telling us the general set-up here.'

'Well, as you know, Mr Pelling owns these Mansions. He lived in the flat next door and we looked after him. Been here some five years, we have, I used to be in the printing trade, but I was made redundant and we got this job through an advert.'

'You've looked after Mr Pelling, as you put it, all that time?'

'We have. Of course, I'm the caretaker of this block–'

'So in five years you'll both have got to know Mr Pelling very well? His habits, his visitors, and so on?'

'Yes, and a good man he was to work for, I will say.'

'Obviously, as this is no case of suicide, he had a visitor last night. What do you know about that?'

'Nothing, Inspector. You see, Friday's our evening off. We went to see our son Barry and his wife last night. Barry brought us home just turned eleven. We came in through the front door, which I locked as usual, crossed the hall out yonder' – he gestured with a thumb – 'and so through the door that leads into the flat here. And neither of us saw or heard anything unusual. I've already asked Kathy about that.'

'Let's get this clear. It's a rule you lock the main door about eleven?'

'It is. Mr Pelling's rule. Of course, all the other tenants have keys, in case they're out late.'

'Latch lock, I suppose? And the main door won't be bolted inside. That means anybody who visited here before eleven could leave at any time afterwards. Not much help.'

Mrs Nolan spoke up tremulously. 'When I went in this morning, the lights were still on in Mr Pelling's room.'

'We noticed that, Mrs Nolan. There was a light in the vestibule also. But none in the two bedrooms, the cloakroom nor the bathroom. We'll work that one out later.' Mallin sat back, the legs of his chair scraping on the floor. 'The other tenants, now. Tell us all about them.' He glanced at Lee, saw him turn to a new page in his notebook.

'This side of the hall first,' Nolan recited rapidly. 'First floor. Miss Chantry and Miss Osgood. Retired teachers. Second floor, empty at the moment. Other side, ground floor, Mrs and Mrs Howard. He's an accountant. Above them, Mr Day. Solicitor. Second floor, Mr and Mrs Greenlaw. Young couple, he's an area sales manager for Grandex Products. That's the lot. All hand-picked with good references, Inspector. Mr Pelling always insisted on that.'

Mallin looked at his watch. The call had come in at nine-thirty – he'd already learned that Pelling was no early riser – and he and Lee had reached here at nine forty-five. It was now well past ten.

'Who's likely to be at home just now?'

'All of 'em, I expect, it being Saturday.'

'Right.' Mallin got up and Lee followed his example. 'We'll have to talk to you again, I expect. Meanwhile, Mr Nolan, if the Press boys come around – and they will – refer them to me first, will you?'

The photographer was packing up his gear in the flat when the CID men returned to it by way of the swing door from the Nolans' quarters. The fingerprint men were still busy, and would be for some time yet. Mallin nodded to the two ambulance attendants who were hovering in the doorway of the vestibule.

'You can load your stretcher, lads.' He walked through, with Lee at his heels, into the main hall of the flats. It was patterned in black and white tiles, there was a heavy square table at one side with a letter-rack above it. Opposite the outer doorway was a lift, with stairs climbing up beside it. On the stairs an elderly lady, severely dressed, with gold-rimmed spectacles and tightly-coiffeured white hair, was addressing a uniformed constable in tones which held both authority and aggrieved reproof.

'But I insist on knowing what is taking place here, Officer. You do not seem to appreciate that this is my home, to and from which I have every right to come and go. Yet you stand there and tell me–'

Mallin strode forward, holding up a large hand.

'The constable is carrying out my orders, madam. There has been a sudden death here and I am the investigating officer in charge. Detective Inspector Mallin.' He waved the

152

hand. 'My assistant, Detective Sergeant Lee.'

The lady allowed herself to relax. 'This is an entirely different matter, Inspector. I have always made it a rule, throughout my years of service in the teaching profession, to assist police enquiries whenever this has proved necessary.'

'In that case, madam, if you would be good enough to return to your flat, we would like to talk to you there.' A commotion at the doorway, where a second constable was standing, caused him to glance over his shoulder. 'Or, at least, Sergeant Lee will have a word with you. Press,' he muttered to Lee. 'I'd better go and sort them out.'

Lee mounted the stairs behind the elderly lady. She addressed no word to him until they reached the first-floor landing, where she turned towards a door which carried a slotted card in a panel. Over her shoulder Lee read, 'Miss G. Chantry. Miss H. Osgood.' She opened the door and invited him in.

The flat was a replica in size and layout of Pelling's, though the furnishings were less exotic, more old-fashioned. The main room was scrupulously neat, there was a long range of crowded bookshelves, a large-screen colour television. And everywhere, on windowsills, shelves, ledges and small tables, were potted plants in profusion.

Lee's conductor was large and well-fleshed, but the lady, also elderly, who rose with a look of surprise from an easy chair with the morning paper in her hands, was slightly-built, fragile-looking. Lee saw she wore a hearing aid.

'I,' said the first lady – and she spoke loudly and distinctly – 'am Miss Chantry. Hilda, allow me to introduce Detective Sergeant Lee. Detective Sergeant Lee, Miss Osgood. And,' she added less formally, 'you'll have to speak up. Miss Osgood is rather deaf.'

Lee acknowledged the introduction with a polished bow. He felt it was expected of him. Miss Osgood goggled at him while Miss Chantry, having seated herself, waved him gracefully to follow her example.

'Now,' she said, 'and what is this all about, pray?'

Lee told them of Louis Pelling's death and the manner of it. Miss Chantry tut-tutted loudly and her friend said what a terrible thing to happen, only, as one might say, a floorboard and a skin of plaster below.

'We are overwhelmed with shock,' Miss Chantry said. 'We also grieve at the passing of a man who has ever been a courteous and accommodating landlord. This is indeed a blow.'

'I'm here to ask you,' Lee said, 'if you saw or heard anything last night which could give us a clue to Mr Pelling's killer. Dr Lazenby, the police surgeon who has already examined him, is of the opinion the shot was fired between eight o'clock and midnight.'

'We saw and heard nothing during that period,' Miss Chantry answered, 'except what the television screen had to offer us. And we turned that off a ten-thirty, which is our normal time for retiring.'

'These flats are sound-proofed,' Miss Osgood added. She spoke in a high, nervous voice. 'Which is fortunate for me with my disability. It allows us to have the television turned up rather high, without being a nuisance to the other tenants.'

Lee knew a dead end when he met one. He got up, thanked the ladies and rejoined Mallin, who was descending the stairs from the flat above.

'Any luck, Bonny?'

'None, sir. None at all.'

'Me neither. I've seen the Howards on the ground floor and the Greenlaws on the second. Also the Days on this floor. I got them all together in a bunch, but nobody could help. So you set a couple of the chaps visiting the other blocks, will you? Then we'll take another look around Pelling's place.'

They asked Nolan to join them. Mallin crossed to the handsome desk, its surface still smeared darkly, and picked up the plastic envelope in which he had previously placed the contents of the pockets of the suit Pelling had worn. Holding the envelope in his hand, he spoke to Nolan.

'Tell us what sort of life Mr Pelling lived here. Did he do much entertaining, for instance?'

'Not in what you'd call a social way, Inspector. He met his friends, I believe, at his various clubs and that. He'd do his entertaining at hotels. Of course, he did bring a friend back here now and then to stay the night. But that was no business of ours.'

'You're speaking of women friends, of course. The same one always, or a succession?'

Nolan grinned. 'You'll have to ask Kathy about that. She kept a sort of check. Lipstick smears, odd bits of clothing left, that sort of thing. I've gathered from her that the boss wasn't keen to tie himself up to anyone in particular.'

'Men visitors?'

'Not very often, to my knowledge. The odd one in for a drink, and, I suppose, a business talk. But you do realize that people could come in here without us knowing anything about them?'

Mallin nodded and shook the contents of the envelope on to the desk. A slim wallet, handkerchief, keys, loose change, a small pearl-handled pocketknife. Clearly, Pelling had been a non-smoker who didn't believe in spoiling the set of his expensive suit by bulging its pockets.

Mallin had previously examined the wallet. It had told him nothing he wanted to know. He picked up the ring of keys, tried the powder-smeared handles of the desk drawers. The long upper one slid out freely, the rest were locked. He found a key which fitted them, turned the locks one after another. Lee lifted the drawers out and stacked them on the desk.

Five minutes examination showed the drawers contained manilla files only, each neatly labelled, all relating to the various business enterprises Pelling had run. There wasn't a single piece of paper among the lot which could be called personal and private. The long top drawer merely held pens,

157

pencils and various other items of stationery.

Mallin sighed. 'Thank heaven we don't have to go into that collection. The accounts lads will have a happy time diving into it, though.' Lee fitted the drawers back and Mallin relocked them. He put the keyring into his pocket.

'We haven't searched the rest of the flat yet. Which was his bedroom?'

Nolan gestured at one of the doors which led off the main room. Mallin took a quick look inside and waved Lee forward. 'You do this one over, while I take the others.'

Lee walked into a room which at once struck a pang of envy into his heart. He was no sybarite, but he liked luxury and perfect personal appointments, as well as the next man. The utility furnishings of his own modest bedroom made it a slum compared to the rich carpeting, the palatial form and accessories of bed, dressing table, chest of drawers. There was a green bedside telephone, a portable colour television set, a soiled-linen basket of gilded weave. The dressing table set of brushes, comb and clothes brush was ebony backed and monogrammed in silver. A revolving stand held a collection of modern novels, all in hardbacks. There was a tang of haircream, male toilet water and after shave in the air.

Lee sighed, a wry admittance that such luxuriousness would never be attained on a policeman's pay. He turned to one of the two fitted wardrobes and opened its doors.

As he had expected, the clothes inside were immaculate – two dinner suits, lounge and casual wear, sports clothes which showed Pelling's interest in golf and yachting. Footwear was treed on two lower shelves. Lee went through the clothes rapidly but found only empty pockets.

The second wardrobe was smaller, it held a selection of overcoats and headgear, with one or two dark-coloured business suits. In the inside pocket of one of them Lee discovered a diary of the current year. He flicked through it. It seemed to carry notes of business appointments only. Then, in a section headed 'Memoranda,' his eye caught two names. Venner. Dawson. And they were bracketed together.

The rest of the bedroom yielded only negative evidence. Lee went out into the main room and heard Mallin's voice in the hall.

The inspector was addressing one of the plainclothes men.

'You're sure you can't pin her down to

anything more definite?'

'Absolutely sure, sir. A smallish, squarish man, arrived in a car about ten-fifteen. Had what looked like a handkerchief or scarf round his head. Came into this building, she didn't see him come out or drive away.'

'A woman in one of the other flat blocks,' Mallin explained to Lee. 'Saw this fellow – no hard identification, of course. There never is. We'll have to check the block again, find out if any of the tenants had a visitor then. If not, this chap might be our man. You have any luck?'

'I found this, sir.' Lee produced the diary. Mallin's heavy eyebrows rose as he read the names his sergeant pointed out. 'Now, I wonder... I think you'd be well employed following this up. Go and see Trent first. Mr Trott's notifying all Pelling's other managers – at his gaming clubs and betting shops and at that road-house he owned. He's asking them down to HQ for a conference. I'll ring back and tell him he can miss out Trent, as you'll be seeing him. Call in at HQ on the way and look at Aston's report of last night. Hadn't time to show it you this morning before this job blew up. I'll carry on here for a while.'

Lee extricated his car from the vehicles

which still crowded the forecourt of the Mansions. At Central he found Aston's report on Mallin's desk. He read it with care and a great deal of interest, feeling certain that Venner's young female visitor had been Marion Kershaw. She had struck Lee as the type who would want to find out things for herself.

Raymond Trent was listed in the phone book with the High Swing number and a private one. Lee noted down the address of the latter.

Chapter Ten

It took a second ring at the suburban bungalow with its neglected front garden before Lee heard shuffling footsteps and the withdrawal of bolts and a chain. Then the door opened and Trent was peering at him through sleep-rimmed eyes. He wore a thick dressing gown and slippers, his swarthy cheeks were black-stubbled, his mouth ill-tempered.

'What the hell!' he exploded. 'Look, this is my home. If you've got any more business with me – and I can't see why you should have – I'd be glad if you'd leave it till–'

Lee cut in smoothly. 'I'm sorry to have to disturb you, sir. But it's very necessary, believe me. Your employer, Mr Pelling, was killed last night in his flat.'

Trent's heavy jaw dropped, he stared open-mouthed at Lee. Unless he rated the Actor of the Year, this was news which certainly had hit him for six. He swallowed hard and got himself under control enough to mutter, 'Oh, my God!' His hand shook as he gestured. 'Better come in, Sergeant.'

Lee followed him through a small square hall into an untidy, unaired room which smelt of stale smoke and staler perfume. Trent pointed to a chair and went forward to switch on an electric fire to boost the central heating. He sat down and at once got up again.

'Let's have it, then,' he said. 'The wife's out at the shops, we shan't be interrupted.'

Lee gave him the essential facts, a summary of which, he knew, would be almost identical with the Press release Mallin had handed out.

'Hell!' Trent said. 'This is going to mess things up proper. I know the boss had turned his affairs into a limited company, but he wasn't married, you know, and he'd no relations. Question is, what's going to happen now?'

'Nothing, with regard to his business concerns, for quite some time, I should imagine, Mr Trent. So you can stop worrying about your job at the High Swing for the moment. I've questions to ask you.'

'Reckon you have. So carry on, eh?'

'The old routine one first. Can you think of any reason why Mr Pelling should have been killed? Any enemies, to your knowledge?'

'None. But you've got to realize, Sergeant, that he and I weren't bosom pals, by any manner of means. I met him at a promotion do when the Fidex people were trying to boost the disc sales of the Moonlighters. Didn't work out, that group just hadn't got what it takes. Thing is, over a drink with the boss I let out I was running a disc and secondhand paperback shop over Almondston way, he needed a new manager for the Swing and he offered me the job. I sold up and took it. But I never saw him out of business hours. And always at the Swing.'

'Of course, you can account for your own movements last night?' Lee's tone was casual.

'You mean...?' Trent laughed hoarsely. 'Look, mate, I've got a good job and I had a good boss. But if you must have it spelt out, I closed up at eleven last night as usual. I was never off the Swing premises all evening. I drove home here – takes me twenty minutes when the traffic's light – found the wife and three of the neighbours just finishing a bridge game. It's a regular Friday night do they have. Arthur Carpenter, his wife and her brother that lives with them. You can check that.'

'I won't waste my time on it, sir. Have you ever possessed any firearms?'

'Never. I wouldn't know a Colt from a – a Luger.'

'Good. Now, Mr Pelling visited the High Swing regularly. Did he ever meet Wilfred Dawson there?'

'The bloke as got killed? Never, as far as I'm aware.'

'What about Dr Venner?'

'Oh, him?' Trent's voice held scorn. 'That nut? You mean, did Mr Pelling know him? Well, they met a couple of times in my office. Venner, of course, explained why he was there – to study our type of client. The boss was rather amused, I thought, but then Venner started on his Down With Everything sermon, and Mr Pelling soon shut him up. Said he didn't believe in that clap-trap.'

'Last Wednesday afternoon I asked you about Dawson, who'd claimed to be a personal friend of yours. You denied this. Do you happen to know if Venner and Dawson were acquainted?'

Trent cleared his throat huskily. 'Look, Mr Lee. When I said I didn't know Dawson, except by sight, that was Gawd's truth. But you asking about him made me a bit curious and I got talking to a few of the regulars and I found one or two who knew Dawson slightly. It seems he and Venner had quite a lot to say to each other when the prof came in, and this Dawson, he told these others he'd been to school with Venner. 'Course, they just reckoned that was another of his lies.'

'I see. That could be checked, of course, but I wouldn't say it's very important.'

Trent smacked a palm on his knee. 'Damn and blast it! I can't take it in even yet. The boss being killed, I mean. God I wish I could get my hands on the bastard who did it!'

Lee levered himself out of his chair. 'That's our job, Mr Trent, and believe me, we're going to work on it. Thanks for your help – I'm sorry I had to disturb you.'

'I'm glad you did as it happens. Even if it was to tell me such news. Sooner I had it, the better.' He moved to the door to show Lee out. 'Knocked me all over everywhere, this has.'

Lee turned on the doorstep. 'Oh, just one other thing. The last time I saw you at the High Swing, you had Sammy Gale with you. You know him well?'

Trent's eyes narrowed. 'What you mean is, what was he doing in my office? The answer to that is, he was looking for a job. Any sort of job. He thought my boss, with all his

166

business concerns, could use an extra man in some way – driver, maintenance man and so on. I used to know Sammy slightly in the old days, when I owned that grotty shop I told you about. He got the idea I could put in a word for him to Mr Pelling. Which I could have done.' He shrugged his wide shoulders. 'No chance of that now.'

Lee wished him good morning and took a cross-town route to Ellerby Close, since it was highly unlikely the university staff would be working on a Saturday morning. He parked his Viva outside Venner's house, walked smartly along the drive and rang the bell. It was answered by the dumpy bespectacled woman with the hair waterfalls whom he had seen in silhouette the previous Thursday evening from across the road.

'Good morning,' he said, and presented his warrant card. She took it, peered at it myopically. Early thirties, Lee thought, and she'd been a pretty girl once. Still could be, if she took trouble. 'Is Dr Venner in?' he asked.

'He is, but he's up in his study. I was told he didn't want any interruptions this morning.'

There was more than a trace of the Benfield accent in her voice. She smiled at him uncertainly.

'This really is important, I assure you, madam. And I won't keep him long.'

'You'd better come in, then' He stepped into a hall with only a crowded coatrack to break its bareness, though its parquet floor shone with polish, its white paint glistened spotlessly. She waved him into the room with the bay window he had previously observed, said she would ask her husband to come down and shuffled away on loose slippers.

The room was wall-to-wall carpeted in grey with a faint rust-coloured motif. There was a lightweight three piece suite, a piano, a cabinet which held glassware and china. An oval table in Swedish wood took up most of the centre. As in the hall, everything was shop-bright, shining and clean almost to a pint of discomfort. A case here, Lee thought, of a personally-untidy housewife with an ultra-tidy house.

The door opened and Venner bounced in. He wore brown slacks and a bright red, high-necked jersey, which, with his fuzzy upstanding hair, gave him the appearance of a cock robin in a high wind. He thrust out a hand and pumped Lee's enthusiastically, cutting off the visitor's apologies for disturbing him.

'Not to worry, Sarge. Old Jim's always available to his pals. I read it you've come about what happened here last night? Bags of bods all over the scene and one of your minions doing his thing – or trying to. They got away, and why not? If whatever it was they were up to was their way towards liberty–'

Lee held up a hand and grinned. 'No theories this morning, please. And I'm not here in connection with your last night's activities.' He straightened his face. 'No, Dr Venner. My business with you is much more serious. You know Mr Louis Pelling?'

'I've met the bastard. Dirty capitalist type to his grasping finger-ends. Somebody ought to shoot that cat.'

'Somebody did so. Last night. In his flat.'

Venner burst out in a cackle of laughter. 'Well, how's that for a wish fulfilled on the spot? So there's one less enemy to revolution in the world! Sarge, boy, we ought to have a drink together to celebrate. I'll just call–'

'No, sir. And I've no time for horsing around. I'd be obliged if you will answer the questions I must put to you.'

Venner shrugged sulkily. 'Oh, well, if you're going to take that attitude... You'd better sit down.' He waved to one of the armchairs and perched himself on the other.

'You needn't ask any questions, chum. I met Pelling a couple of times at the Swing. Casually. We didn't get on. That's all I know of the swine.'

'A diary has been found, sir, belonging to Pelling. It has your name in it, bracketed with that of Wilfred Dawson. Could you possibly explain that?'

Venner put up a hand and rubbed at his side whiskers. 'Just a minute...' He was serious now. 'I seem to recall – ah, yes. The second time I ran across Pelling at the Swing, we left Trent's office together. I went to have a few words with some of the boys and girls who were hanging around. I saw Dawson accost Pelling in the foyer, they spoke together for a while – maybe two minutes or so. And I saw Pelling take what could have been a diary out of his pocket and write in it. That may be some sort of explanation – it's all I can offer.'

'I asked you last Thursday morning, Dr Venner, how well you knew Dawson. You said you had met him, and talked to him, some half-dozen times at the High Swing. I then asked you if you had had anything to do with him outside that place, you said you hadn't. No, wait a moment!' He put up a hand as Venner opened his mouth protestingly. 'I have no reason to disbelieve you. But Dawson put it around that you and he had been at school together. Was that true?'

Venner nodded. 'Perfectly true. It didn't seem relevant, so I didn't bring it up when I talked to you. I was some three years senior to him, we were both scholars at Farley Street school for a while. I left when I won what in those days was called a scholarship. I went from grammar school to university.'

'Dawson, of course, would remind you of those days during your conversation with him?'

'Yes, he brought the subject up. You know the sort of thing – do you remember? Followed by a list of schoolboys and staff, most of whom I'd completely forgotten.'

'Was Mr Holder mentioned, by any chance?'

'Old Gripper, as we used to call him? Why, sure.' Venner smiled, quite warmly. 'Most popular master on the staff. And could he use a cane when it was necessary? But only when a lad deserved it.'

Lee resisted the temptation of commenting that, it seemed, Venner's views on the value of discipline had obviously changed over the years. 'There's just one more question, sir. We have to put it to everyone, indiscriminately, who knew Mr Pelling. Will you give me an account of your movements last night, please?'

Venner laughed harshly. 'Movements? Chum, I was practically static. At half past seven a woman student from the university visited me by appointment. She left about ten minutes past eight. Almost immediately after, the plainclothes policeman called. I suppose you know all about that?'

'Yes, I've read his report.'

'Right, then. I came back into the house, had a stiff whisky to settle my nerves after the hoo-ha, my wife and I ate supper. She went to bed. She hasn't been sleeping well lately, so she took a couple of the pills her doctor prescribed. That would be about half-past nine. I went to my study and worked there till midnight. I then sought my couch, as they say. Satisfied?'

While he had been speaking, Lee had heard the hall telephone ring, and Mrs Venner answering it. Now she came into the room, said, 'Excuse me, please, but there is a call for Detective Sergeant Lee.'

'Thanks.' Lee got up and went to the instrument. He announced himself and heard Mallin's voice. 'Thought I might catch you there. Get anything special out of Trent?'

'Nothing which seems important at the moment. Just a couple of odd facts... He has a watertight alibi, I'd say.'

'Venner too?'

Lee repeated what Venner had told him and Mallin said, 'Listen,' and talked for a full minute. When he had done, Lee replaced the handset on its studs and went back to join Venner. Mrs Venner had returned to the kitchen regions.

'That was my superior, Detective Inspector Mallin, sir,' Lee said. 'Information has been brought in which concerns those movements of yours last night. A story which doesn't coincide with your own. Mr Mallin would like you to go to Central to sort it all out.'

Venner sprang up, his jaw set, his brows drawn together.

'You mean–? You're telling me somebody's making me out to be a liar? Here, just what is this all about?'

'I don't know the precise details, sir. But Inspector Mallin would be grateful if you'd talk to him, as soon as possible.'

'And suppose I refuse to do so?'

Lee shrugged. 'It's up to you, sir. We can't make you – at the moment. We'll just have to proceed on this information received, which would cause you inconvenience, to say the least.'

'Then I'll talk to your inspector on the telephone.'

'Which wouldn't be satisfactory, sir. I know this is breaking into your time, but it would be best if you'd co-operate.'

Venner walked across the room to face Lee. His fists were clenched, his face a picture of fury.

'You, your inspector and the rest of the Fascist pigs can go to hell!' His deep voice was level, but it was loaded with anger.

'Very good, sir.' Lee turned away at once. 'I'll give Inspector Mallin your message.' He walked out of the house, closing the front door behind him. He drove his car slowly to the top of Ellerby Close, turned there and drove back. He was almost opposite Venner's house again when its owner came hurrying along the drive, struggling into his anorak. He gave a shout to attract Lee's attention and came up to the car when Lee pulled it to a stop.

'I've reconsidered.' His tone was brittle. 'I'd like to get this business settled. My car is too unreliable to drive at the moment. I take it you will give me transport?'

'Certainly, sir.' Lee leaned sideways to open the passenger's door and Venner got in, slamming the door with a violence which made Lee cringe in sympathy for the Viva de Luxe.

They exchanged only a few casual words on the journey to Central. Lee noted that his passenger showed no inclination to fall back into his 'with it' role of speech. The man had shed all signs of his former trendiness. Could that be because he was now extremely scared?'

Chapter Eleven

Alfred Grover, Assistant Chief Constable of Benfield, was tall and broad, with a heavy thatch of greying hair and a florid, weathered complexion which could have been that of a farmer. At sight, he seemed to be a solid, equable type of man, in actuality he was fussy, easily put out by trifles. He was a fairly new appointment by the Watch Committee, and Superintendent Trott, who found him difficult to please, had a shrewd idea that Grovers touchiness was due to an inner uncertainty as to whether he could hold down his job.

Trott and Mallin had been summoned to the ACC's room, a place of opulence and space which made their own offices seem like backyard dog kennels. Grover hadn't asked them to sit down. He frowned up at them from behind his elegantly-appointed desk, blinking his grey eyes rapidly, a habit he had when things weren't going to his satisfaction.

Trott, who had been urged to present a

progress report, had done so with the uncomfortable feeling that it was a case of a few words and no progress at all.

'So.' Grover fiddled with a blotter. 'You have seen these various managers of Pelling's concerns and none of them can help us.' He picked up a copy of the medical report Trott had furnished and blinked at it. 'Death before midnight... M'm... Fairly definite for once. Bullet recovered, Ballistics suggest a Walther PPK as the weapon. Same as that used in the Dawson shooting,' he added quickly, before Trott could remind him. 'So we proceed on the theory that the two cases are linked. Hey?' He shot the question between them.

'That's reasonable, sir,' Trott agreed. 'Mr Mallin, as you know, has set the investigation going. We are doing everything possible.'

'I should hope so. Now, this diary business. The two names. Venner and Dawson. Lee, you tell me, is following it up. You did not consider, Mr Mallin, that it was important enough for your own personal attention? Dr Venner holds a high place at the university, you know.'

'Sergeant Lee is quite capable, sir. Also, as my previous report to you states, he has already interviewed Venner in connection with the Dawson business.'

'Of course, of course.' Grover straightened the blotter again. 'Well, it seems we must proceed along the usual lines, but with energy and dispatch. Remember that, gentlemen. And don't fail to get the message over to your men. Every one of them.'

The two said a simultaneous, 'Very good, sir,' and left the ACC to his meditations. Outside, Trott expelled a long breath. Mallin nodded, there was no need for words between them.

They walked down to the ground floor. 'I'll just check any reports which may have come in,' Trott was beginning, when a constable from the front office hurried up to them.

'Excuse me, sir, but we've got two lads wanting to see Sergeant Lee – or you, sir,' he added to Mallin. 'They say it's about the shooting at Ashcroft House.'

'I'll see them in my office now.' Mallin turned to the superintendent. 'You want to be in on this, sir?'

'Not unless it turns out to be really important.' Trott was in the throes of one of his gloomy fits. 'Which it probably won't.'

Mallin said to the constable, 'Bring them to my room.' He went ahead, settled himself in the chair behind his desk. There was nothing in the way of information on the desk, only a series of progress reports (though progress was hardly the word) from the men still working in Ashcroft House and its neighbourhood. The constable came through the door, ushering two teenage boys. One was tall, thin and spotty-faced, with small, mean-looking eyes and uncared-for hair brushing his shoulders. He wore an old army tunic, the inevitable jeans and shoes which had once been black. He slouched in with an air of faintly-amused superiority which caused Mallin's toes to tingle. His companion was chiefly notable for a shock of bright red hair above a freckled face and large green eyes which stared out upon the world with an innocence too good to be real. His upper garment was a lumber jacket several sizes too big for his short, pudgy body.

'Ralph Jowett and Timothy Baker, sir.' The constable set wooden chairs in front of Mallin's desk, nodded the pair into them and went out.

Mallin leaned back, surveying his visitors.

'I know you, Jowett, of course,' he said. 'Going straight now, I hope?'

'Look, mate.' At nineteen, and with a sizeable amount of juvenile form to his credit, Ralph Jowett didn't mean to be patronized. 'We ain't come here for no sermons. We bin sent here by Ray Trent. You know him, then?'

'Manager at the High Swing. Carry on.'

'Well, it's this cat Venner, y'see, as works at the university and Mr Pelling, what's got shot, he didn't sorta trust him and so he gets Ray to set us on – that's me and Tim here, along with Ted Crabshaw and Jackie Green and Vince Lane – to keep an eye on him. So last night–'

'Just a minute. Let me get this straight. How did you know Mr Pelling had been shot? The evening papers aren't out yet.'

Jowett waved a pair of grimy hands impatiently. 'Ray Trent told me. We was on this watching act last night an' the night before. And then I had to call Ray on the blower this morning. At his pad, like to report. Which I done and Ray drops me that word about Mr Pelling. Now can I get on?'

'Presently. You say Mr Pelling didn't trust Dr Venner. Why – do you know ?'

'I asked Ray Trent that, when he passed me the word to get the gang cracking on this scene. "Mr Pelling reckons Venner's a dangerous type," Ray ses, "and he wants to find out what he's up to, who visits him, all that." Right. So when I make the tinkle to Ray just now, and tell him, he ses, "Ralph, boy, this is one for the fuzz. So grease the skates and head for Central. Tell all to Sergeant Lee, or his boss if he ain't there.'

'So you tell me.'

'Which is what we come to do, eh, Tim? If you'll give me a chance.' He wriggled in his chair. 'It's like this. Me and my group we drive to this Ellerby Close in Jackie Green's banger and we leave Jackie parked near by. Night before last, this is. We slide in and case Venner's pad. Orders is, watch from eight to ten. We work a sorta scheme with two of us each side the house. We c'n see front and back that way. Nothing happens for a bit, except a fuzz car looking round the house opposite, like. Then a big bloke comes along and parks himself in the porch of this empty house, which it must have bin empty becos of the fuzz car and you c'n allus tell by that, eh? Are you with me?'

Mallin nodded and Timothy Baker said, 'Reckoned, we did, the bloke were going to do a tickle there. Vince Lane, he said it wasn't a bad idea, and mebbe we could–'

'He was having you on,' Jowett said quickly. 'And I'm spilling it, aren't I? So mute the trumpet, eh?'

'Get on with it,' Mallin said wearily.

'This guy did nowt but stand there. Must have bin waiting for a bird what didn't turn up. Any road, who should appear on the scene but a coupla guys what I know and in they go to this Venner's. They was there over half an hour. In the front room only we couldn't listen under the winder becos of this character across the street. He'd'a' seen us and our orders was to keep outa sight. When these two guys went, so did this feller. Lights soon went out in Venner's pad and we come away.

'Okay. So I buzzed Ray next morning and give him the griff. Later we go to the High Swing and was told to carry on last night as before.'

'You told Trent about seeing Sam Gale and Edwin White going to Dr Venner's house?'

'Hey! How the 'ell did you know–'

'I said that big bloke across the street looked like a cop, didn't I?' Baker broke in triumphantly. 'I said at the time–'

'Aw, can it!' Jowett growled. 'Well, last night–'

It was Mallin's turn to interrupt. 'I know about that. I had another man watching the house. He saw you four go into the garden

182

and disappear round the back. He helped Dr Venner to flush you, you got away. Is there anything more?'

'You bet there's more, mister! We come back a bit later, see? When your bloke had gone home. Right. There's a light in one of the upstairs rooms at the back. And a ladder and Tim here shins up and looks in the winder. No curtain, see? You take it now, pal.'

Baker nodded. 'It's a sorta study spot. Lotsa books and papers and that. And this Venner's knelt down in one corner with the carpet turned back and he's feeling about there. Then he lifts up a floorboard and puts his hand under and brings out a gun. I mean, a pistol, sorta. I see him get some ammo from this place, an' all, and he loads this gun. Then I comes down this ladder quick.'

'We only just managed to get yon ladder back inta the garage,' Jowett said, 'when Venner comes out, gets inta his car and drives off. We're a bit puzzled how to go on now, so I ring up Ray from a call box and he ses a coupla you wait on till Venner gets back and then pack it up. So this me and Tim did.'

'And he left – when?' Mallin looked up from the notes he was making.

'Let's see, now. It was around nine when

Venner and your bloke chased us off. We got back on the job 'bout a quarter to ten. I reckon it was something like twenty past when this Venner drove off. He was back at half-eleven – I know that for sure because I checked me watch. He put the car away and we reckon he went straight to bed becos the lights was all put out soon after and at that we come away.'

Mallin got up. 'Hang on a minute, will you?' He called a constable to take charge and went out to use the telephone in the front office. When he returned he sat down behind his desk again, motioning the constable to stay. Baker was staring stolidly before him, but Jowett didn't appear to be so sure of himself now. His feet were shifting on the worn carpet of the office, the fingers of one hand were beating a tattoo on his knee.

Mallin grinned at him sourly. 'Beginning to wish you'd never come here, lad?'

Jowett shrugged. ''Tisn't that. Nicks allus give me that creepy feeling – you know.'

Mallin didn't comment on this. He looked sternly at Baker.

'You agree that what Jowett's just told me is the truth?'

'Sure I do. Every bit of it. Oh, I know we was trespassing, as you might say, but

184

there's no harm in that, is there?'

'Listen carefully,' Mallin told them. 'You realize, don't you, that you've made some very serious statements about Dr Venner? And that Mr Trent wouldn't have told you to come here if Mr Pelling hadn't been killed – by shooting?'

Jowett shrugged. 'Sure. We're telling you what Ray Trent thinks, I guess – that this Venner did Mr Pelling in last night.'

'You're both prepared to sign written statements of what you've told me?'

'Well, yes, I suppose so.' Jowett exchanged a doubtful look with his friend.

'And that, unless those statements can be proved to the hilt, you could be in serious trouble for making them?'

Jowett drew in a long breath. 'Look, mister, we done what we was told to do. So you take it from there, eh?'

'If you'll both go with the constable, then. He'll take you to a room where you can either dictate your statements or write them down yourselves.

When the youths had gone he turned to the telephone directory. He looked up Trent's home number, asked the station exchanged for an outside line and dialled.

'Detective Inspector Mallin, Central

Police Station,' he announced when Trent answered his ring. 'I've just had a couple of youths to see me, sir. They came, they said, on your instructions.'

'That's right.' Trent sounded eager, co-operative. 'They told you the tale about what happened last night?'

'They gave me a long and involved story concerning Dr Venner. Is it true they have been watching his house on your instructions?'

'Not mine. Mr Pelling's. I told them to make that clear to you. I merely–'

'That's all right, sir. I was just confirming. Is it also correct that you know why Mr Pelling gave those orders?'

'It is. I haven't any idea what his object was.' He paused, and his accented voice held a note of regret as he added, 'And maybe we'll never know now. When Mr Pelling gave orders, Inspector, a wise man jumped to them if he wanted to keep his job. I did just that.'

'You've had Sergeant Lee to see you this morning?'

'That's so. He hadn't been gone more than a few minutes when young Jowett rang me. Otherwise I'd have told Mr Lee what Jowett had said. I told him – Jowett, that is

– to get in touch with you at once. If Venner–' He broke the sentence off.

'Mr Trent, have you any idea why Dr Venner and Mr Pelling should be – well at odds, let's say?'

'Absolutely none. They met here and they didn't think much of each other. That was my impression, anyway. But...'

Mallin said, 'Thanks. I've no doubt we'll be getting in touch with you again.' He put the telephone down and said, 'Yes? Come in,' as a knock sounded on the door.

Lee and Venner entered. Mallin and the professor were introduced. Venner was given a chair. The inspector regarded Venner closely, coolly. He didn't much like what he saw though he reminded himself that he was an old-fashioned type, with a bias against modern trendiness. But he accepted some of the words in fashion and there was one which came to his mind now. Uptightness. It was clear Venner was suffering from an attack of this.

Mallin opened the interview on a casual, friendly note.

'I appreciate your coming here, Dr Venner. We are, as you know, slaves of routine and regulations. We're also busy people, rushed at the moment with a couple of homicides on our hands. So when we're able to cut through those regulations and that routine because someone like yourself is co-operative, we are duly grateful.'

Venner licked his lips and frowned. 'Couldn't we scrub the yak and get to the main business?'

'Certainly. You know why Sergeant Lee visited you this morning. You gave him an account of your movements last night, I know. You told him, after the detective constable and yourself had routed those four youths, that you didn't leave the house again. But the youths tell me they returned later and watched your premises. And that you did go out, in your car. At some time between a quarter past and half past ten. You deny this?'

'Judas Priest! Of course not, so why should I? It's quite true.' He raised both hands in a placating gesture as Lee and Mallin began to speak simultaneously.

'Just give me a chance to explain, will you? When my wife went to bed, I decided to work in my study. But I had not got down to it long before I remembered there was an important letter I had to finish. I did this – and I can give you the name and address of my correspondent and a summary of the contents of the letter, if you wish. I wanted this letter to catch the first collection in the morning. So I took it, in my car, to our nearest post office, which is over half a mile away from my house. Now, it's true I didn't tell Sergeant Lee I had done this. I told him I had gone to my study and worked until midnight. But, before I could relate how that work had been interrupted by my recollection of the letter I mentioned, he was called to my telephone and I was requested to come here. You'll agree, Sergeant?'

'Yes, sir. The call did interrupt us at that point.'

'Fair enough,' Mallin responded. 'You went in your car to post the letter. To a post office half a mile away. How long did that take you? Five minutes at most?'

Venner grinned. 'It took me over an hour, comrade. The car started up okay, though I noticed the dashboard panel warning light for the ignition didn't go out as it should have done when I started the engine. The car faltered once or twice on the way to the post office, and the engine died on me just short of my objective. At that time of night – I ask you! Now, I'm no mechanic, but I couldn't just be stuck there, you know. So I got under the bonnet and fiddled about a bit and after an age or two I found a broken wire, twisted the ends together, shoved a piece of insulating tape around one and all, and off she started. And went for about a hundred yards before she died again. More fiddling, found I hadn't made a good connection, put this right and we got home.'

He leaned back in his chair, very much more relaxed now then he sat upright to add, 'I can't produce witnesses, of course. One or two people did go by while I was working on the car, but I spoke to none of them and I got no offers of help.'

'So that clears up one point,' Mallin said. 'And it seems the youths were speaking truth there. Now, about these four. They say they were watching your house on the orders of Mr Louis Pelling. Their assignment was to report on your movements and your visitors. It was not explained to them why they were to do this. Can you help us here, Dr Venner?'

'I've absolutely no idea. No idea whatsoever. I can't imagine why Pelling was interested in me at all. We met twice, briefly, at the High Swing. We had nothing – but nothing – in common.'

'Yet he seems to have thought you were worth keeping an eye on,' Mallin said musingly. 'And nobody appears to know why,

190

not even Trent, through whom the boys received their orders. You know Trent pretty well, I believe?'

'I visit the High Swing fairly regularly in connection with the field work I am doing.'

'It was at the High Swing where you met Samuel Gale and White?'

Venner laughed boisterously. 'Oh, good God, no! I dropped across Sammy in Cranley Jail. Did one or two visits there as a research project. After all, I am a sociologist. I get around to these spots. He seemed a bit forthcoming, ready to wag the old tongue in the way I wanted. I asked him to come and see me, for further chat, when he got out. So he turned up the other evening and brought another cat with him. Chalky White. We had quite a scene – it lit me up.' Lee noted he was trying, with no particular success, to get into his old act again. He added abruptly, 'Hey, how do you know about that? About Windy and Chalky rolling up to my pad?'

'Things get around,' Mallin replied, and grinned. 'Dr Venner, you've been very helpful. We had to check on the story these youths told us. They're not the type whose word you take without question. I'll see you get transport home, sir.'

Chapter Twelve

When Lee returned to Mallin's office after seeing Venner out he found the police constable who had been sent off with Jowett and Baker standing by Mallin's desk.

'Right,' Mallin was saying. 'Turn 'em loose. You've got their addresses.' When the constable went out, Mallin handed Lee the statement Baker had made. 'Cast an eye over that, Bonny.'

Lee's lips were pursed in a soundless whistle before he reached the end of the misspelt but quite legibly-written sheets.

'If this about the gun under the floorboard is true, sir, it suggests Venner as Pelling's killer. Dawson's, too, since the same weapon seems to have been used in both cases.'

'Yeah.' Mallin was looking doubtful. 'The period Venner was away from home, allegedly with a car breakdown. If that was a lie he'd have had time to drive to Pelling's flat and back. But there is a snag.'

'You mean, it's Venner's word against this boy's?'

'That's it. Venner could deny what Baker says he saw, unless we could find the Walther in Venner's possession If the thing came to court, the word of a back street tearaway wouldn't have much chance against that of Dr Venner, MA, PhD.'

'You didn't mention Baker's story to Venner just now, sir, when you spoke of the four who watched his house.'

'That was deliberate, of course. We haven't anything like enough proof to slap a charge on Venner. Search warrant to turn over his place? If we found nothing we'd be right in the sewage.'

'And I'll bet, if we take a look at his car, sir, we'll find that broken wire taped up, as he said. He wouldn't have trotted out a yarn like that unless it could be checked, which we might decide to do. And he did mention to me that his car had been acting up.'

Mallin nodded. 'You didn't meet Jowett and Baker just now,' he said. 'Jowett's all blabber and impudence, but Baker – well, he's a quieter type. I'm wondering if he really did see what he claims he did, or whether he made that bit up... He could have seen something rather odd and used his imagination on it. By the time he got down that ladder, the something could have

193

been a gun and ammunition in his mind.'

'I've seen Trent this morning, as you know, sir. He didn't tell me anything about these boys and their activities, though this statement says they were set on to watch Venner by Trent on Pelling's orders.'

'I rang him about that. He agreed he'd done so because Pelling wanted it. Apparently you had left before Jowett rang in with his report to Trent. Trent told him to bring Baker here to tell us what they'd seen. Did you get anything from him?'

'He seemed to be knocked endways when he heard Pelling had been killed. He was clearly worried as to how this would affect him and his job. But two rather odd points emerged. I asked him if he possessed any firearms and he said no, and added he wouldn't know a Colt from a Luger. I suppose, to the ordinary man, the words "firearms" is associated with hand-guns, but still I hadn't told him what Pelling had been shot with, you see.

'The other point was that Trent told me Dawson and Venner had been at school together. I put this to Venner when I was interviewing him and he confirmed it. They were at Farley Street. Holder taught them both. Probably this is not the slightest bit significant.'

'M'm.' Mallin considered. 'Mr Trott's gone out to dive into Pelling's background, with the ACC hot on his heels. I'd better get back to Ashcroft House, see if there's anything more I can do there. The chaps I left on the spot haven't come up with anything yet. Suppose you run out and have another talk with Holder? He might be able to tie Venner and Dawson up a bit more closely for us.'

Lee emitted his usual, 'Very good, sir,' and having made sure by a telephone call that Holder was at home, he drove to Dainford Road. It was a mild, almost sticky morning and Holder's neighbours were making the most of it. Cars were being washed, gardens tidied for the coming winter. A typical suburban Saturday morning scene, Lee reflected, as he parked the Viva outside number 20.

He was warmly received by Holder – he guessed this working-with-the-police business had put a real glow into the retired schoolmaster's placid life – he was taken into the sittingroom and given a comfortable chair. He refused coffee, sherry and beer.

'I won't keep you long, sir,' he promised. 'We're still working on the Dawson case, of course, but nothing has turned up yet, we've not even been able to find anybody whom the Press can describe as helping with our enquiries. It has been a matter of digging away into Dawson's background in the hope we'll strike some sort of oil. Now, you told us he was a former scholar of yours. I believe you taught James Venner at Farley Street, also?'

Beneath his thatch of white hair, Holder's eyes lit up.

'Ah, Jim Venner. As the phrase has it, I have watched his career with interest. He now has a professorship at the university here. Did you know that?'

Lee smiled. 'I have talked to him briefly about his schooldays. He had some very nice things to say about you.'

'Holder gave vent to a sardonic sniff. 'You surprise me, Sergeant. Venner and I were constantly at odds. He was a great trouble-maker.'

'In what way, sir?'

The old schoolmaster's eyes were hooded now as he looked back at the past.

'He was what one could call a stirrer-up. He kept out of bother himself, but he delighted in setting it going, between his schoolmates, between them and the staff. A wise guy, a smart Alec, as we said in those days. And very hard to catch at his subversive activities.

'But the lad had brains – no doubt about that. In my own opinion, at that time, he would use them in later life in one of two ways. He would turn out to be quite a brilliant scholar, or a very clever crook. I'm glad the weight eventually fell on the right side of the fence. He passed into grammar school and there he seemed to settle down, though I did hear he had one or two brushes with authority before he finally came to his senses. From there on he climbed rapidly.'

'Leader type of material, was he?'

'You could say that. Unfortunately, at Farley Street he led the younger, less worthy types. The real lads, the tough guys – and we had our share of them, believe me – wouldn't look at him, except to boot his backside occasionally, for his own good. Boys are very perceptive, you know. Good judges of character But I'm vastly intrigued as to why you are asking me all these questions about Venner.'

'As I said, sir, it's a matter of backgrounding Dawson. Was he one of Venner's followers?'

'He certainly was. They were never in the

same class, for Venner was two or three years older than Dawson. But I remember the younger boy almost hero-worshipped Venner when they were at Farley Street and was completely dominated by him.'

'In those days, you say, Venner was against authority. Was Dawson in that category, too?'

'Great Heavens above – no! He hadn't the guts. Nor the brains... You know, I've been thinking about him a lot. At school he wasn't altogether a likeable lad, he told lies frequently, he was lazy at his work. But his home life was pretty grim and one couldn't help feeling sorry for him. I tried to help him all I could, though it did go against the grain sometimes. One had to be careful or he would take advantage.' He looked up at Lee. 'I'm sure I'm not furthering your investigations very much.'

'Every little helps,' Lee said tritely, since he could think of no other reply. He felt he had learned something of the characters both of James Venner and Wilfred Dawson. He could visualize the latter, meeting Venner again at the High Swing, trying desperately to cash in on their former acquaintance, as a status symbol he could take for himself. And Venner giving him the brush-off... Unless

Dawson in Venner's eyes, could be useful material... Yes, that was possible, too.

He took his leave of the Holders and drove back into the city. It was time, his stomach reminded him, that he had his lunch, and he intended to relax over it. Between them, Mallin, Trott and the ACC could deal with the Pelling job at the moment; he himself, more eager to follow up the case of Dawson, and convinced now that Venner was an important link, decided he would see what Marion Kershaw had learnt, if anything, when she had visited Venner on the previous Thursday evening. With a little luck, he might find the girl at home this Saturday afternoon.

Mrs Kershaw opened the door of 14 Canal Road to his knock. Her expression, when she saw who it was, said plainly, 'Oh, lord, you again?' but she forced a smile to her lined face.

Lee apologized profusely for troubling her. 'I wondered if your daughter was at home, ma'am. If so, I'd like a word with her.'

The smile was replaced by a worried frown.

'We'm just having our dinner – lunch, I mean – in the kitchen. And everywhere's in a bit of a mess, an' all. Sat'day's our cleaning day, you see, when Marion can be at home to help me.'

'No problem, Mrs Kershaw. I'll wait in my car. Tell Marion to finish her lunch in peace and then she can join me there.'

'Right.' She was relieved at once. 'I'll do that, then.'

Marion kept him waiting less than ten minutes. As she got into the car, wearing a dark red jumper and navy slacks, she brought a pleasing wave of scent with her. Lee saw she had freshly made up; he took this, accurately enough, as a tribute to his own masculinity.

'Sorry about this,' she said, smiling at him. 'But as mum has told you, we're domestic slaves on a Saturday morning. However, I'm free now. And in no rush. Roger Ineson's a write-off on Saturday afternoons in winter. Rugby football is his mistress then.'

'You don't go to watch him play?' Lee wanted to lead into this interview casually. Marion mustn't get the idea his visit was of overwhelming importance. He needed her to be relaxed, to talk easily to him.

'The idea of shivering on a touchline in a wet and muddy field while thirty fellows commit mayhem on each other isn't my idea of fun, Mr Lee. And if I meet him on a

Saturday night he's far too tired, too played out, to be – well, really exciting.' She smiled mischievously.

'So we've time to talk, Marion.' He put on a mock-official air. 'It has come to my notice that, despite your former castigations of Dr James Venner, made in my presence, you have recently visited him at his home. I would appreciate an explanation.'

She turned towards him, her eyes widening. 'Who told you that? Roger?'

'Not Roger. Let's leave it at "information received," eh?'

'Mr Lee, I've become interested in Dr Venner. In his ideas, rather. I've talked to a number of people at the university who are particular friends of his and I don't like the poison he's spitting around. Anarchy through student power – all that. It's dangerous.'

'But not new. And, surely, it's taken up by only a very small percentage of your fellow-students? Isn't it true, also, that most young people have ultra-Left Wing leanings at nineteen or twenty, only to shake these off a year or two later? I know this happened to me.'

'Yes, but you've got to realize there's a difference nowadays. Once, you couldn't go to university unless you could measure up to a really high standard. There weren't the places available. Now, practically anybody can get in. There's a poorer type with us now. They've been spoon-fed all their lives, they'll swallow any muck. And when you get the sort of stuff Venner pours out...' She shrugged her shoulders and gave him a smile of apology. 'Sorry. I'm letting myself be carried away.'

'You went to see Dr Venner at his house, Lee reminded her.

'Yes. I first saw him at his room at the university. I pretended to be interested in what I'd heard of his ideas. I wanted to get them at first hand, you see, though I didn't tell him that. He saw me as a potential disciple and he opened the floodgates. But he'd an appointment that afternoon, and I couldn't stay. He asked me to go to his house for a further talk in the evening. Roger ran me up there, waited for me. He didn't think much of the idea.'

'And did anything come out of that visit?'

'Only a cup of very inferior coffee, made by his wife, and a lot of hot air from him. He tried to impress on me that his movement, as he called it, was growing both in depth and in distance. He told me he'd been down at Colton University recently, talking to the Students' Union there and that he'd had a most heartwarming reception.'

'Depth as well as distance,' Lee repeated musingly. 'What was that supposed to mean?'

'That all types of people, even outside the universities, were keen on joining the movement. He instances some fellow he'd met at the High Swing, a former schoolmate, who wanted to come in, offered to help with the financial side, too. Venner thought this was screamingly funny, since the chap proposed, with Venner's help, to run a blackmailing job on some fellow where he worked. Said he could get the evidence if Venner would come in with him. Venner wouldn't touch it, he said. And I think he was speaking the truth there, for once.'

Chapter Thirteen

Here and there, in every police force, you can still find the old-fashioned bobby. He is a slow, deliberate type, usually elderly as police officers go, almost always of constable rank only. He is unambitious, unimaginative, but he pulls his weight and can be depended upon. He accepts the amalgamation of Forces, the regional crime squads, the transceiver he carries in his tunic's upper pocket, as essential parts of the modern age, in the same way as he accepts his wife's demand for a washing machine and her championship of the long-haired, scrubby-looking young fellow his daughter intends to marry. But he doesn't like them.

Police Constable Albert Henson was one of these. He was grey-haired and portly, his face red and seamed. His uniform was always meticulously brushed and tidy, his buttons, his badges and his boots shone dazzlingly even on the dirtiest of days.

Bert Henson was also a soccer fan and he worshipped at the shrine of Benfield

United. When the roster had instructed him to report for duty this Saturday afternoon at Horseferry Road, United's ground, for the needle match with Coalford Town, hope had risen high that he would be assigned to inside-the-ground patrol. It would likely mean having to deal with odd spots of trouble, but he'd see the game. However, the super in charge had other ideas. To his disgust, Henson had been given a duty in Horseferry Road, outside the ground.

He stood, disconsolately, opposite one of the turnstiles, watching the trickle of late-comers hurrying along, hoping they'd get there before the gates were closed. The side of the road which faced the long, high wall of the ground was occupied by two factories, a warehouse and an abandoned church, with small shops dotted here and there between them. All the shops were closed, their doors and windows barricaded with stout wooden baulks. The companies with whom the shop-holders were insured had insisted on this when Benfield United were playing at home. Henson only hoped there'd be a bit of trouble to deal with when the match was over and the crowds came streaming out. He'd welcome the chance of getting rid of some of his frustration by tackling a few of the bovver boys.

A newspaper seller standing by the turn-stile entrance with his bundle of the lunchtime edition of the Benfield Evening Chronicle was displaying a placard – 'Homicide of Prominent Benfield Business-man.' 'Louis Pelling,' he'd told Henson hoarsely when the policeman had strolled across earlier. 'Shot through the head.' Henson couldn't care less. He'd heard of Pelling, of course. Most everybody in Benfield knew the bloke by name.

A sudden roar from inside the ground marked the appearance on the field of the rival teams. Sourly, Henson turned to look again at the dwindling stream of men, women and boys anxiously pounding along towards the gates. A small man amongst them, almost entirely enveloped in a large scarf of United's colours and with a huge rosette pinned to his lapel, turned away from the rest and disappeared into a narrow passageway between two of the shuttered shops. Had Henson's eyes not been focussed in that direction he would never have noticed the man's deviation from the others. Of course, the fellow could have legitimate business there, though it seemed odd that he should choose such a time for it. A keen supporter of United would have one object in mind – to get the other side of those turnstiles before they showed the 'Ground Full' boards.

Henson strolled slowly towards the passageway. It ended, as he could see, in a yard which served both of the shops. At the far side of the yard were the backs of the houses in the next street.

On one side of the passage was a small hardware and do-it-yourself store, on the other a tobacconist's and confectioner's. The latter had done a roaring trade among the football fans until, just before kick-off, the owner had closed the premises. Henson walked down the passage and into the yard. It was empty.

Long-standing habit made him glance at the doors and windows at the rear of both shops. The back door of the tobacconist's was slightly ajar. Henson went forward and at once saw the marks of the tommy bar which had forced it. He stood outside the door for a few moments, listening. He thought he could hear a man's voice raised in a note of shrillness, somewhere inside the house.

He pushed the back door open, with his gloved hand and stepped into a tiny scullery.

Another door, closed, led towards the front premises. He went to this door and now he could hear plainly.

'You just do what I say, missis, and nobody gets hurt. You go inta that shop and you clear the till. And when I says clear it, I mean just that. Me, I'm standing in the doorway yonder while you do this. Any funny business, and the old man gets a slug in the guts. You an' all if you try owt.'

'You dirty rotten little crook!' That was a woman's voice, thick with fury. 'If I could only get my hands on you, just for one minute– Oh, thank God!'

Her gratitude was triggered by the sight of Henson's large figure. He had opened the inner door quietly and now he stepped into the scene.

It was a warm, comfortably-furnished sittingroom with a gas fire glowing in the hearth. An elderly man sat rigid in an armchair, his hands, with the finger joints knotted and swollen, feebly clutching the chair arms. He seemed to be struggling, ineffectually, to rise. Beside him, in an attitude half of protection, half of defiance, stood a very large grey-haired woman, her face crimson with anger and shock. And facing them was the small man whom Henson had seen going into the passage. At the woman's exclamation he wheeled round, and Henson's quick glance saw that the pistol he held in his hand was merely an elaborate and very accurately-fashioned toy.

The little man emitted a squeak of alarm as he took in Henson's looming figure. The policeman stepped forward, chopped at the man's wrist and kicked his feet from under him in one smooth co-ordinated movement. As he fell, the woman dropped to her knees beside him, seized his ears and began banging his head, in a fit of fury, against the carpeted floor. Henson picked up the toy pistol which had fallen from the man's hand and pocketed it. He took his time over the process.

The would-be bandit began to yell for help. The woman had one knee pressed into his stomach and showed no signs of giving up her attack. Henson spoke quietly to her.

'Pack it in now, missus. He's had enough. Better let me take over, eh?'

She struggled to her feet, panting. Henson grabbed a handful of grimy shirt and hauled the little man to his feet.

'Thought I'd seen you before, chummy. White– Chalky White – that's you, isn't it?'

White put up a shaking hand to feel

tenderly at his ears.

'Look,' he gasped. 'I didn't mean no harm – I swear I didn't. I was only having a bit of a game. I mean' – he looked wildly around – 'I was just pretending – for kicks.'

'Which you'll get, right up the backside,' Henson promised, 'if you don't sit down in the chair yonder and keep as still as death.' He helped White towards the chair with a hefty push, and turned to the woman. 'Now, then, Mrs–?'

'Slater, that's us.' She jerked her head. 'Me hubby there is crippled with arthritis, I run the shop. I'd closed up, because of the match, and we was settling down here when this – this worm come busting in at the back and threatened all sorts if I didn't give him all we've got. Ee! I'd like to get at him again! Can't I, just for a couple of minutes?'

Henson grinned at her. 'We'll leave him to the magistrates. Let's see – breaking and entering with intent to rob, demanding money with menaces, having an offensive weapon on his person. That'll do for a start. I'll just get in touch with my super now. This thing' – he tapped his transceiver – 'will likely work better in your backyard than here. Shan't be a minute, but you keep an eye on him, Mrs Slater, and if he moves so

210

much as a muscle, I'll add resisting the police in the carrying out of their duties to the charges.'

He gave his report concisely over the air and was told to hang on till one of the patrol cars which were standing by arrived to take White to the local nick. 'And then,' the superintendent added, 'you can come into the ground, Henson, and report to me at the North Stand entrance. I can do with a few extra men inside here.'

'Yes, sir!' Henson responded. The Fates were not entirely against him, after all.

Edwin White was duly escorted to Horseferry Road Station, where, a watchful eye being kept on him, he waited until after the match, until Henson came along to charge him. United had won handsomely, Henson had had a splendid view of the game, he regarded Chalky White almost paternally as, in his role of arresting officer, he went through the formalities. But Chalky had not been idle while he had sat on that hard bench in the Horseferry Road nick, sipping the regulation mug of tea which had been brought him. He had been thinking deeply. It had proved hard work as he mentally reckoned up various pros and cons, but he had stuck to it manfully and was now prepared to do a deal for himself.

'Now you've got that off'n yer hairy chest,' he said sourly to Henson, 'just you listen to me. I got important information about this Pelling as was croaked last night. I don't haveta spill it, and you can't make me, but if I was to, it might help me with this other job, eh?'

'That depends.' The station sergeant, who was standing by, didn't seem impressed. 'You'll probably make it all up, anyway.'

'On me sacred oath, I won't! I know who done Pelling, see? But I'm not telling none of you here. I'll talk to the bloke as is in charge of that job, and not to nobody else. And if you don't let me, it'll be the worse for you!'

The sergeant reached for a ring of keys. 'Take him down and put him away, Bert,' he told Henson wearily. 'That'll give him a chance to think up a few more fairy tales.'

But, as White was led protestingly away, the sergeant lifted a telephone and called CID at Benfield Central.

He was put through to Mallin who, with two murder cases still on his hands, had no thought of weekend time off. He listened to what the sergeant had to say, asked a couple of questions and said he would be at Horseferry Road inside the next twenty minutes.

So in due course White was taken from the cell where he had been dumped and escorted to the station's interview room. Mellin, seated at the table there, looked up.

'Right, Chalky,' he grunted. 'Sit down and spill it – fast.'

'First off, Mr Mallin, I gotta be sure it's going to do me a bit of good over this job what I was fingered for 's afternoon.'

'That depends on what you have to tell me. I don't make promises, nor bargains.'

White sighed. 'You're a hard man, Mr Mallin. But say I could name the bloke as killed Pelling, you'd speak up for me?'

'Maybe. If you weren't making up some daft yarn.'

'It's Gawd's truth, Mr Mallin. Mind you, I didn't exactly see the job done but I knew it was going to be done and by who.'

'Accessory before the act, eh?' Mallin spoke testily. It looked as if he were wasting his time here. White waved his hands.

'No, nothing like that! Don't get me wrong. Becos when this chap said he'd like to do Pelling, and would if he got the chance, I just thought he was sorta joking.' He saw the impatient gleam in Mallin's eye and went on hurriedly.

'Thursday night, as it happened, me and a pal went visiting.'

'You and Sam Gale called on Dr Venner, in Ellerby Close.'

White gaped at him. 'How the flamin' 'ell d'you know that?'

'Never mind. Just go on with the story. Why did you go there?'

'He asked us to. Leastways, he asked Windy to call an' see him and Windy took me along, us being pals, like.'

'How did he get to know Gale?'

'Through Ray Trent at the High Swing where he goes now and then. Windy and Ray, they're sorta cousins, see? And Dr Venner, he knew Windy had bin done once or twice by you blokes and he reckoned he was an interestin' case to study. That's what Windy told me, anyroad.

'So we go there in Windy's banger and this Venner sits us down and gives us a beer apiece and then he starts talking – and how! Me, I couldn't get half of it, all about destroying the Establishment and recreating – I think that was the word – a new world outa the ashes of the old. Sorta stuff you hear these Commies spouting in Greenside Park on a Sunday morning, on'y they're just shooting off their mouths and this bloke

214

Venner – well, Mr Mallin, he meant it. Got hisself worked up till he started to scare me, I c'n tell you. He went on about as how we'd have to get rid of the police first, then the big business lot, for instance, Louis Pelling. He said Pelling was an evil influence in any society and that he hisself 'ud cheerfully shoot Pelling, given the chance. However, in the end he come to why he'd asked Windy up there. He said he'd got a lotta students on his side, all over the country, and they'd form the nuke – summat. I've forgot the word.'

'Nucleus?' Mallin suggested.

'That's it. Of his fighting forces, he said. But they were on'y kids in the main and when this thing of his started he'd want some real tough guys to lead 'em, to be his officers, like. Guys that knew their way about and wouldn't be above smashing a few heads in. Guys like Windy and me and any of our pals we could get to join up. Well, Windy says we'd have to think all that over and do a bit of planning, like, and then we come away and when we gets outside Windy ses to me, "I'm having nowt to do with that bloody nut, Chalky," he ses, "becos he's dangerous," and I ses, "You couldn't be righter."'

He sat back in his chair and let out a long breath.

'So,' Mallin said harshly, 'just because Venner sounded off about Pelling, among others, and Pelling gets killed, you're telling me Venner did it? You bring me down here just to waste my time, eh? And you have the all-fired cheek to imagine this'll help you over the charge you're in here for?' Irritatedly, he pushed back his chair and got to his feet.

'But that isn't all, Mr Mallin,' White said anxiously. 'I mean, I got more evidence than that. If you'll just listen…'

Mallin saw the little man meant it. 'Get on, then.'

'On the way home, in Windy's old car, Mr Mallin, he started on about Louis Pelling. He'd been up to Pelling's pad a coupla times – them flats, you know. And Windy, he ses what marvellous pickings there must be there if a bloke felt like having a go.

'Well, that got me thinking, I must say. And so – I don't like telling you this Mr Mallin, but I got to – last night I went along to these Belle Vue Mansions, just to have me a look around. That was all – I swear it. And I'm doing this when a car drives in so I get me inta a dark corner, outa sight. A fellow steps outa this car and the light shines on his pan and I see it's Venner. Only, he's got a sorta scarf tied round his bonce, to cover all that sticking-out hair of his, I reckon. And in he goes to Ashcroft House, where Mr Pelling lived. I stuck around and he came out about five minutes later. That was at eleven. I heard a church clock strike.'

'You can swear to all this White? You're sure it was Venner you saw?'

'Pos'tive. I can give you the number of his car.'

'One other question.' The thought of collaboration in stories was in Mallin's mind. 'Do you know a lad called Jowett, or any of his friends?'

Chalky shook his head firmly. 'Niver heard of 'em, Mr Mallin.'

Chapter Fourteen

It was a working Saturday for Lee also. On his way back from talking to Marion Kershaw about Dr Venner, he had stopped at a favourite Italian restaurant for lunch before returning to Central. He found Trott and Mallin there, gloomily kicking around the few facts they had on the Pelling case and not scoring with them. They both looked hopefully at Lee.

'I've seen Holder again,' he told them, and I got some general background both on Dawson and Venner. Dawson, it seems, was trying to suck up to Venner on the strength of their former schooldays. We didn't check Venner's alibi for the night Dawson was killed, did we?'

'Hell, no!' Mallin exploded. 'Why should we? At the time, I mean. Though it might be worthwhile, if this story that Venner possessed a gun is true. Trouble is, can we rely on that young Baker? He could have imagined that gun, or simply made up the story. We've got his statement for what it's worth, but…' He sniffed loudly. 'And as for an alibi, Venner could make one up easily enough. "I was at home all night, ask my wife." That sort of thing if he couldn't provide a better one.'

'Yes, sir. I've also seen Miss Kershaw and I've picked up rather an odd piece of information from her.'

He told them of Venner's story to Marion that a former schoolmate, met at the High Swing, had offered to increase Venner's fighting funds by blackmailing, with Venner's help, a man for whom he worked. 'This must have been Dawson,' Lee said. 'And since Dawson worked only at the Nortons' and for Langton and Wells, the scrap-metal dealers … Dawson, it seems, wanted Venner to help him to get the blackmail evidence. Miss Kershaw said he, Venner, just laughed at the idea.'

'All the same,' Trott said shrewdly, 'you'd like to follow it up, eh?'

'I think it's worth it, sir,' Mallin put in. 'And I'd begin at the Nortons'. Langton and Wells are clean, there's nothing Dawson could have got at there. They've enough business to keep out of illegal scrap deals, even if they felt like it.'

Trott sighed. 'Very well. See what you can

dig up Lee. I'm going back to Pelling's place. I'll leave you in charge here, Tom.'

'Plenty of paperwork to do,' Mallin responded, 'and I hope I don't get any interruptions, either.' He was not to know then that Chalky White would put a firecracker under that hope.

Lee drew up outside 50 Dainford Way and found Julian Norton in his front garden. He was wearing an old mac, a battered trilby and thick tweed trousers thrust into gumboots. His hands were gloved and a wheelbarrow on the path was half full of rose clippings. He looked up as the Viva stopped, and waved a pair of secateurs when Lee got out of the car.

'Good afternoon, Sergeant!' He walked down to the gate. 'I trust you haven't come to see my wife? She's helping at a rummage sale this afternoon at St Mark's Church Hall. Won't be back for long enough.'

'It's you I wanted a word with, sir. Though you seem to be busy, too.'

'Just shortening these roses a bit. They've made a lot of wood growth this year. I'm not a believer in autumn pruning but these need cutting back. Prevents a lot of wind-rock during the winter, you know.' He heaved a sigh. 'It's a job poor young Dawson was

220

going to do, but… Anyway, I was intending to pack it in. My spinal trouble won't let me do much at once. I'll just wheel this lot round to the back and we'll go in by way of the kitchen. Might be a good idea to drink a cup of tea there, eh? I usually have one about now.'

The kitchen was warm and comfortable, Lee sat on a wooden chair and watched the dark-haired, tubby little man move quickly around, putting the kettle on to boil, setting cups and saucers and a plate of chocolate biscuits on a brightly-patterned tray. 'That's about right, I think,' Norton said. 'Ah, milk and sugar, of course. What have you on your mind, Sergeant?' He offered Lee the biscuits and when his visitor declined, he stuffed one into his own mouth and chewed at it greedily. 'I oughtn't to, I know.' He patted his heavy paunch. 'Can't resist 'em, though. But I was asking you…?'

'We've been talking to some of Dawson's acquaintances and friends, Mr Norton. And an odd piece of information has turned up. Dawson told a certain person that he knew of a way to run a blackmail racket at the place where he worked. We've been wondering if he meant this place, sir.'

'Good God!' Norton had taken a second

biscuit. It snapped in his fingers but he seemed unaware of this. 'You can't possibly mean it was Dawson who...' Lee saw the effort he made to alter the sentence. '...who would dream up such a damn fool idea? I know he was an outrageous liar, but that – why, it's ridiculous!'

'You mean there was nothing here he could have used as a matter for blackmail?' At Norton's quick headshake Lee added, 'Your wife talked to him a lot. Could she have possibly let out something – say some matter connected with your business – which Dawson could have thought of as a source of extortion?'

'That's unthinkable, Sergeant.' Norton dropped the remainder of his biscuit on to the tray and moved to a shelf from which he took a teapot and caddy. 'I have never discussed business with my wife,' he said over his shoulder. 'In any case, we're a straightforward, ordinary company. We have no valuable trade secrets or anything of the sort.'

The kettle was boiling, he carried the teapot to it and poured. The teapot lid rattled as he put it into place.

'You'll forgive me, sir, if I ask whether Mrs Norton had any personal secret which

Dawson might have wormed out of her?'

Norton laughed shrilly. He came back to the kitchen table and sat down opposite Lee.

'This conversation is getting more and more absurd, Sergeant. But we can leave my wife entirely out of it. There was nothing Dawson could have got out of her. I'd swear my life on that.'

He jumped up again, seized a spoon and began to stir the tea leaves in the pot vigorously. He brought the pot to the table, sat down again.

'Milk and sugar?'

'Milk only, thanks.' Lee was watching Norton closely. He saw how the man's plump fingers were shaking as he picked up the milk jug, how jerkily he spooned sugar, over generously, into his own cup. He reached for the teapot but Lee stretched out an arm to forestall him.

'Better let me do that, sir. Your nerves seem to be somewhat upset.'

'I – er–' Norton's protest died. He watched Lee pour the tea, staring at the stream of liquid as if he were fascinated by it. Lee put the pot on its mat and spoke quietly.

'It's this talk of blackmail which has disturbed you, isn't it? Blackmail's the dirtiest word in my book – in any policeman's book. And, liar though he may have been, I don't think Dawson would have made that statement if it had been entirely untrue. Therefore, I'll just have to follow it up from the other end, see the informant again and put him through the story exhaustively. He may come up with some small piece of knowledge he has temporarily forgotten.'

Lee's eyes had never left the other man's face and he now saw the distinct crumbling of Norton's defences. 'In this way,' he went on, 'the truth will come out, not perhaps in a pleasant manner, but–'

'That's enough!' Norton flung up his hands. 'You've sold me the idea.' His voice was shaky but determined now. 'I'll tell you everything.' He picked up his cup and sipped at it. Lee saw his hands were steadier as he returned the cup to the saucer.

'Two years ago I had this spinal injury. The pain was intense, really shocking. I've always been a bit of a coward about physical suffering and I went through hell with this. The hospital treatment wasn't exactly pleasant, either. And the doctors told me that, though they could eventually take the pain away, I must consider myself, with regard to my spine, as a semi-invalid for the rest of my days. This was mentally shattering, too.

'My wife, Sergeant, is a fine woman, and we've been very happy together. But she doesn't understand physical suffering, never having had any herself. She didn't realize that at that time I needed sympathy, extra tenderness. I don't blame her, it wasn't in her nature, you see.

'There was one of the nurses at the hospital, more than twenty years younger than myself, but she seemed attracted. She gave me all the extra attention, the kindness, my wife couldn't give. And I suppose I was flattered that such a lovely young woman had singled me out.' He looked up at Lee and grinned crookedly. 'I'm making quite a meal of this, I know, but I do want you to understand.'

'You carry on, sir. Get everything off your mind.'

'I fell heavily, crazily in love with her, and she seemed to return my feelings. When I left hospital I wrote her a number of very passionate letters. She replied once or twice, then stopped. I tried to contact her at the hospital but she had left there suddenly and nobody seemed to know where she had gone. I've never seen nor heard of her since.'

225

'But somebody got hold of the letters you wrote to her and has been blackmailing you – or she could have done it herself?'

Norton nodded glumly. 'I received a letter marked "personal" at my office when I got back to work there. It contained photostat copies of my letters and a promise to hand the originals over a down payment of fifty pounds. I couldn't face the alternative mentioned, that further copies would be sent to my wife. That could have broken up our marriage completely. My wife never would have forgiven me. So I paid up.'

'But you didn't get the originals back, of course?'

Norton shook his head. 'It was always a case of just one more payment and I'd really get them. Oh, I know I've been a fool, but I've gone on hoping, and paying out, over the past eighteen months. To the tune of something like five hundred pounds.'

Lee finished his tea, put down his cup and sat forward.

'Right, Mr Norton.' He spoke crisply. 'So let's get this thing sorted out. And stopped. Who has been blacking you?'

'I don't know. After the first demand, I received a phone call at the office. A man's voice, obviously disguised, said something

226

like, "You've got my letter with the photo-copies? Now listen carefully." He told me I must take fifty pounds, in used notes, after dark that night to Dainford Common. That's some half mile from here, you know, I must put the money in a certain litter bin. I must go alone and return home as soon as I had deposited the money. The following night, at the same time, the letters would be found in the same bin. If I alerted the police, or brought anyone with me, or failed to carry out instructions, I would be attacked, sooner or later, in such a way that my spine would be damaged irreparably.

'I think, Sergeant, that last threat affected me most. I just could not face another period of agony and suffering. I took the money as instructed, and went eagerly, the following night, to recover my letters.'

He shrugged. 'I suppose it was idiotic to expect they would be there. I heard nothing more for over a month. Then the man rang again. He said there had been what he called a slip-up over returning the letters, but this time, for an additional fifty pounds... And that's how it has been going on. Excuses each time for non-delivery. I've gone on kidding myself that the next time the promise would be kept. You'll think I'm the world's worst fool, I know.'

'You certainly have been unwise, sir. But I do realize what a powerful grip a blackmailer can get on his victim. It happens again and again. But we can put a stop to it, you know. You have no idea at all who this fellow is?'

'Absolutely none. I've always been careful to keep my private life completely separate from my business concerns. Nobody at the works could have discovered my secret. Obviously, the nurse must come into it somewhere, but I've not been able to trace her.'

'So let's consider Dawson as a possibility. He claimed he had a source of blackmail here. From what you've told me, you were that source. Not your wife.'

'But how on earth could he have got hold of those letters? Or have known anything about that stupid affair of mine? Besides...'

'Yes, sir?'

'It's just come to me. On one occasion when I had to deliver the money, Dawson was away from here. He was on holiday in Blackpool.'

'You are certain of that?'

'He rang me up from Blackpool earlier that evening. I'd decided to plant a heather garden here and had discussed it with him.

While on holiday he had come across a nursery with a very fine selection of heathers. He rang to suggest that he bought a number of plants and brought them home with him. We discussed quantities and varieties on the phone. When he returned from holiday he produced the plants, with the nurseryman's labels on them.'

'He could have had a confederate, of course, who picked up the money you left on Common.'

'But I can't see how Dawson could possibly have known... Look, Sergeant, does my wife have to know about all this?'

Before Lee could answer, the door which led from the front part of the house into the kitchen opened. Mrs Norton stood there.

'I already know enough of it to guess the rest,' she said.

Chapter Fifteen

The men sprang to their feet, Lee's action motivated by common courtesy, Norton's by sheer surprise and alarm. Mrs Norton came into the kitchen, pulling her gloves from her plump hands. The purple coat she wore did not, Lee thought, go with her auburn-dyed hair.

'If there's a spare cup of tea in that pot,' she said, 'I'd love it. I'm dying for one.'

'But–' her husband stammered, 'I thought – I mean–'

'You thought I wouldn't be back yet, Julian. But the rummage sale was so successful, such hordes of women turned up looking for bargains, that we sold out in no time. And do sit down again, both of you.'

She drew up a chair for herself while her husband, somewhat shakily, found an extra cup and saucer and poured her tea. She thanked him and said smiling at them both, 'So let's get it all straightened out, shall we?'

Julian Norton said, 'How – how long have you been there listening?'

'Long enough, dear. Not that I learnt a great deal more than I already suspected.'

'I think,' Lee suggested tactfully, 'that you two would prefer to be left alone for a while. I can call back.'

But Mrs Norton shook her head. 'No need for that, Mr Lee. We're not going to have a domestic row over this. I'm glad it's come to the point where it can be cleared up between us.'

She took a long drink from the cup, set it down.

'When Julian came home from hospital, he was in some ways a changed man. He was jumpy, secretive. I knew he wasn't worried about business so I guessed it was another woman. I wanted to tackle him about this, but he was still suffering a good deal of pain and I didn't think it would be fair. As I heard Julian tell you, Mr Lee, I'm afraid I'm not a very sympathetic person with regard to pain and illness. If this other woman could give him what I couldn't, at a time when he needed it – well, all right.'

'That was a very generous attitude, Mrs Norton.'

She shrugged her heavy shoulders. 'I knew it wouldn't last long, and it didn't. But then, later, I realized Julian was particularly worried, every now and then, about something. He would leave the house after dark on the excuse he wanted to go for a walk. Most unlike him.' She turned to her husband. 'One night I followed you dear. I saw you put an envelope into the waste bin on the Common. You walked away back towards home, I had to hurry to get here before you.

'What was in that envelope? A love letter? Somehow I didn't think it could be. You see, I knew you weren't playing me false with another woman then – not any more. Female intuition? Call it that. But I didn't think about blackmail...'

Norton let out a deep breath. 'So it's all right, Grace? I was a fool for a while, I know. But you really forgive me?'

'Of course. I forgave you long ago.'

She turned again to Lee. 'And now you're going to help him to put a stop to this business, aren't you?'

'That depends on who has been blackmailing him, Mrs Norton. He has no clue about this, but it's been suggested to me that Wilfred Dawson had something to do with it.'

Her eyes opened widely. 'But that's absurd! It's crazy!'

'You talked to Dawson quite a lot, didn't

you? Did you ever speak, or even hint to him, about your husband's errands to Dainford Common?'

'Of course not. I–' She bit her words off with a snap of her dentures.

'Yes, Mrs Norton? You've just remembered something?'

'I can't see it's of any importance.'

'You must let me be the judge of that if you want this matter settled.'

'But Wilfred would never have taken advantage. I mean, I only mentioned it for fun.' She frowned uncertainly, began again. 'Look, Wilfred used to do odd jobs for me, apart from his work in the garden, such as cleaning shoes. One day he was doing this and asked where I had been the previous night, as the shoes were very muddy. I said jokingly I had followed my husband to the Common, wondering if he had gone to meet a woman there. That was all.'

'Did Dawson clean your shoes, Mr Norton?'

'I suppose so. Either he or the daily, Mrs Carr.' He looked at his wife who murmured, 'Wilfred.'

'And,' Lee went on, 'you wouldn't normally wear the shoes in which you went to business for the Common?'

'I invariably wore an older pair.'

'The demands for money came at regular intervals?'

'Yes. One every second month and always on the same day – the first of the month.'

'So it's possible that Dawson, if he took care to be observant enough, could have made a note of your Common visits from the state of your shoes?'

'I suppose so, though that seems rather far-fetched to me.'

'True. But it seems Dawson knew you were being blackmailed. It could be – since you are sure he wasn't the blackmailer – that he worked out when your next visit was likely to be and set himself to watch.'

The Nortons looked at each other. It was clear neither of them was sold on the theory. Lee went on quickly.

'Mrs Norton, did you talk to Dawson at all about your husband's stay in hospital?'

'Well, yes, several times. Why not?' She added, to her husband, 'I once showed him that photograph you had taken in the ward just before you were discharged – you know.'

Lee said, 'Have you still got it? I'd like to see it.'

'If you wish.' Mrs Norton rose and went

out of the kitchen. Norton said nervously, 'Another cup of tea, Sergeant?' and when Lee declined he said, 'Think I'll have just one more biscuit.' He chewed away at it until his wife returned.

'Here you are.' She held out a six by four glossy photograph. It showed the interior of a hospital ward with a group of patients and nurses posed against a background of beds. There were enough crutches and plaster casts in evidence to show it was an ortho-paedic ward. Julian Norton was seated in the centre of the group, flanked by a handsome West Indian nurse and a blonde with large eyes and a hard mouth – Norton's light o' love, Lee guessed. She looked the type who could make a man fall for her, and bleed him white afterwards. His glance roved casually over the rest of the group, and was suddenly fixed. He laid the photograph on the table and pointed.

'Do you happen to remember this man's name, sir?'

'Why, sure,' Norton replied. 'We were in adjacent beds and became quite friendly. Though I haven't seen nor heard of him since I left hospital. His name was Raymond Trent.' He gave a small laugh. 'Odd thing, that nurse next to me – not the coloured

235

one, of course – was a sort of second cousin of his. A lucky chance, because he and I got rather preferential treatment as a result.'

Lee pushed his chair back, got to his feet. 'I'd like to borrow this photograph, Mr Norton. It's possible it may put an end to all your recent worries.'

'You mean Trent had something to do with the – the extortion business? I can hardly believe... Though that nurse, his relation, was – er–' He seemed to choke.

Lee took his leave hurriedly. The Nortons, he knew, had a few things to discuss between them, without a third party present.

The November dusk, with a touch of fog in it, was falling quickly when he got into his car. He switched on his sidelights and drove back into town.

He reached the High Swing on the stroke of half-past four. It seemed to be doing excellent business this Saturday afternoon. Raymond Trent was in the vestibule, and he came up to Lee at once.

'Any news, Mr Lee? About Mr Pelling's death, I mean.'

'Enquiries are proceeding, sir. We hope to make an arrest soon.' It was bluff, but even if Trent realized that, it seemed to have no effect on him. He shrugged.

'Good luck to you, anyway. I thought a long time before I opened this place today. Thought I shouldn't, as a mark of respect to the boss. Then it struck me he would have wanted business as usual, which was always his motto.'

'Quite right,' Lee said indifferently. 'But I'm still working on the case of Dawson's death. Could I talk to you in private?'

'We'll go into my office, though I don't see how I can help you any more than I've already done.

'Now,' he said when they were both seated, 'what's it all about?'

'Our ballistics experts are ready to swear the gun which killed Dawson was the same which put an end to Mr Pelling's life.'

Trent took that in open-mouthed. Then, 'You don't say! That should make things easier for you, eh? I mean, same killer for both jobs.'

'It doesn't necessarily follow I believe you knew Julian Norton, for whom Dawson worked part-time as a gardener?'

Trent scratched his dark-shaded chin. 'Julian Norton – would that be the same fellow I met in hospital, I wonder? I was in for a neck injury – some bone or disc or something slipped, couldn't move my head.

Damned painful, it was.'

'Norton set up an affair with one of the nurses. It carried on for some time after he left hospital. Did you know about that?'

'He did seem to be rather keen on Nurse Foster. I tried to warn him off but he'd taken a right toss for her and she seemed like she wanted to play along. What's all this in aid of?'

'I understand Nurse Foster was a relation of yours. I'd like to get in touch with her. Can you help me there?'

Trent was sitting very still, very tense. He took his time in replying.

'She's a second cousin, as it happens. I told her to drop this thing she had going with Norton. But I don't know where she is now. She went to Canada and I've no idea of her address.'

'Yet Norton, over the past eighteen months, has been blackmailed to the tune of five hundred pounds, because of the letters he wrote to this Nurse Foster.'

'I don't know anything about that.' Trent's response was just that little too bit hurried, Lee decided. This was the moment when a copper went in with his head down – and even bent the truth a little.

'The game's up now, anyway,' he said.

'Norton has confessed all, in my presence, to his wife. The letters are so much waste paper in the hands of the person who is holding them. So you might as well put a match to them, Mr Trent.'

Trent stared at him. His tongue came out to wet his lips.

'I don't know what the hell you're talking about!'

'Oh, come now, don't let's play games. Mrs Norton followed her husband to Dainford Common one night. She'd become suspicious of his late walks out. They weren't in character, you see. And she saw enough to blow this racket into bits.'

'That's just damn foolishness. She couldn't have done. I–' His lips clamped together tightly.'

Lee leaned forward. 'Look, though I hate the guts of a blackmailer, I've got a more important job on than running you into the ground because of what you've been doing to Norton. Otherwise you wouldn't be sitting there. You'd be at the nick, with your name on the charge sheet. But Dawson was in this blacking job some how. I want to know all about that.'

He added, 'If you've any sense at all, you'll help me. It's more than likely Norton can be persuaded not to take action against you if I put in the word.'

From beyond the office walls the latest pop hit came muted. Lee forced himself to relax the tensed muscles in his hands and arms. This was the crunch, the crux-point. Trent would either break clean, or he'd clam up completely. There could be no half measures.

Then Trent began to speak, almost in a mumble, and Lee's hopes rose. The suspect who talked high, loud and clear was in most cases, merely spinning a web of lines. Truth more often came from confused, broken sentences.

'You said just now... Before you began on Norton and that ... Louis Pelling was shot by the same gun that did Dawson.' He cleared his throat, he cleared his throat and the words became more distinct. 'I reckon I can give you the name of the fellow who used it. Both times. That nut Venner.'

He glanced up from under his overhanging brows to see how Lee was reacting to that one. The CID man sighed wearily.

'Let's take it all step by step, shall we? If you've anything to say which I can work on, you'll have to make a proper statement later. At the moment, it's all off the record. Let's begin with Dawson.'

'He found out what was going on – about the letters Norton wrote, I mean. He told Venner Mrs Norton had said enough to him to let him guess there was something up. I reckon he worked it out that I was getting in touch with Norton on a regular day every couple of months, and did a bit of spying on that Common. Anyway, he told Venner he'd seen me collect the bread Norton had left one night. And he – Dawson, I mean – wanted in on the job.'

'He went to Venner about this – he didn't tackle you directly?'

'No, for two reasons, I reckon. He knew if he'd said a word to me I'd have had him done over the same I had that sneaking young bastard Kershaw' His lips clamped again.

'Never mind that now. What was the other reason?'

'He also knew he couldn't do anything without some sort of evidence. I'd got the letters Norton wrote, my cousin gave them to me before she left England, but Dawson couldn't get his hands on them. All he could think was that the photo Mrs Norton had shown him – he recognized me on it – might be something to work on, but, you see, the trouble was to get hold of it. He'd found out it was kept in a locked bureau in the Norton's sitting room. When he was in the house, Mrs Norton never let him out of her sight so he couldn't get hold of the photo. But he got what he thought was a brilliant idea. He'd get a pro crook to lift it for him.

'Right. He knew Venner was in touch with Windy Gale and Chalky White. He went to Venner, told him I was blacking Norton, that there was a source of cash which Venner, if he went in with Dawson, could use for his fighting fund for red revolution. Venner pretended to go along with him.

'Dawson's scheme was that Venner should get Chalky, or Windy, or both, to break in at the front of Norton's house while he kept the old dame busy at the back. This would have to be done in an afternoon, when the daily woman wasn't there. The lads would skeleton-key the bureau, lift the photo, hand it to Dawson later. A bloody silly idea, if ever there was one.

'Venner came to me and told me what Dawson had told him. Venner said he wanted in on my game or he'd blow it to you people. We'd keep Dawson out of it, of course. And we'd step up the payment demands. Norton, Venner said, was the sort of industrial boss he was out to get, anyway. Sergeant, suppose you had been me, what would you have done then?'

Lee frowned. 'I think I'd have had sense enough to realize the game was up, when both Dawson and Venner knew of it. I may be wrong, because I don't know how the minds of you filthy blackmailers work.'

Trent raised his hands in protest. 'No need to be like that! I'm coming clean, aren't I? And there was another thing – Venner's idea of putting the screw on harder. That was daft, it 'ud only make Norton stick in his toes, likely. Anyway, look. I've told you all, of my own free will. And I'll send the letters back to Norton at once, and that's on my sacred oath. Thing is, what are you going to do about it?'

'Returning the letters means nothing, Trent. They're no use to you now. And I'm more interested, at the moment, in the claim you made that you knew Venner shot both Dawson and Pelling. That's a very serious charge to make, you know.'

Trent shrugged. 'I can't prove it, naturally. That's your job. All I know is that Venner has, or had, a pistol, a Walther. He showed it to me. He said he was going to scare Dawson with it – tell him to keep out of the

243

game with Norton – or else. What's more, young Baker saw him with a gun last night. He told you that, didn't he, when I sent him to see you this morning? And I know Venner hated Pelling.'

Lee sat for a while staring at Trent. How much could he depend on what the man had told him? Or on what Trent obviously now believed, that Venner was responsible for Pelling's death? There were lots of ifs and buts in Trent's story. And because of these precipitate action might be dangerous. But this went with regard to no action at all, too.

'You're prepared to make a formal statement covering all the information you've given me?' he asked.

'I've got to, haven't I?' He glanced at the watch on his wrist. 'And I'll go with you and do it now, at the nick, if you like. My afternoon customers'll be drifting home and the evening crowd won't be in for a while. I've got a good kid taking Kershaw's place, he can look after things.' He stood up. 'So what are we waiting for?'

Chapter Sixteen

'So,' Superintendent Trott said grumpily, 'we've got two statements, one from White, one from Trent. And both as insurance, as you might say, by their respective makers. White hopes to ease that break-in charge by telling us he saw Venner go into Pelling's flat last night. Trent fingers Venner as Pelling's killer on evidence which wouldn't stand up in Court, Trent's idea being to make us wink at his blackmailing. And how much can we believe from the said statements?'

'Young Baker swore he saw Venner handling a gun,' Mallin put in. He added hastily, 'Don't remind me, sir, that it was Trent who sent the boy to tell that.'

'Yeah. I can see Venner had some sort of motive for killing Pelling, since he seems to have hated his guts. And if we believe White, Venner lied about having trouble with his car. Let's not forget White's tale has some backing, that of the woman who saw a man with what looked like a scarf round his head, going into the flats.'

'So we tackle Venner next?' Mallin suggested. 'Though we haven't enough on him to clout him with a charge?'

Trott picked up a pencil from his desk, began to chew the end of it, shook his head as if he didn't like the taste, And put the pencil down. He spoke to Lee, who was sitting next to Mallin.

'You've left Trent at that High Swing place, eh? I suppose there's no likelihood he'll cut and run somewhere?'

'Danby is keeping an eye on him, sir, watching his car. I thought that precaution would cover things for the moment. If Trent does make a break, he'll do it on wheels.'

'Good.' Trott reached out for a telephone. 'I'm going to ring the ACC. He won't like being disturbed on a Saturday evening, but this is one time he earns his brass. He can make the decision on what we do about Venner.'

Three minutes later, having said his piece and listened, he broke the connection with a 'Very good, sir. Yes, we'll keep in touch.' He turned to the others. 'Grover's a trifle scared in case we handle Venner too harshly – his word, by the way. If these allegations we have are false, Venner could make big trouble. I agree with him there, of course.

The way things are at the moment this has got to be a kid glove job. But Grover agrees Venner must be seen immediately and he suggests that you, Lee, take him on. Get over there and if he's at home, chat him up. You've talked to him a couple of times recently and when you turn up again, he won't likely think a lot of it. We won't warn him you're on the way, but, in case he does say anything of use, you'd better have somebody with you. Witness, and all that. Aston's on stand-by, take him.'

Lee told Detective Constable Aston the details of their assignment as he drove the Viva to Ellerby Close. 'I read your report on the obbo you did on Venner's place last night, Dave,' he said. 'You met Venner. What were your impressions of him?'

'We weren't together long enough for me to reckon him up in any sort of definite way. There was one odd incident, though. When those lads made a rush for the gate and disappeared, they apparently knocked Venner down on the way. At least, that's what he said when I found him on all fours on the lawn by the drive. He grabbed me as I was running past, as if he wanted helping up, and that delayed me just enough to let the kids get away. Venner said one of the lads had a cosh, and hit him a glancing blow with it.

'When Jowett and Baker came in this morning I went into the interview room where they were making their statements. I asked Jowett about that cosh. And he said, "Don't be bloody silly, mate. We hadn't none of us any offensive weapons on our persons. Why should we? We was set on to watch this university cat, we wasn't going to a football match!"'

Lee grinned. 'Anything else?'

'I asked which one of them had knocked Venner down. I was curious, you see. Jowett said nobody had touched him, that he had dodged out of the way and dropped on the grass. That could have been a lie, of course.

'But it makes you wonder, Dave, if he suspected Jowett's gang had seen something which he, Venner, didn't want them to tell us about.'

He steered the car into Ellerby Close and drew up outside Venner's house.

'You'll stay in the car, Dave. Keep your head down until I get into the house – there are lights on, so it looks as if somebody is at home. I want Venner to think I've come alone, as I've already told you. If I need you, I'll call you in. And when I do, remember to lock up and bring the car keys with you. I don't want some bright lad taking this baby for a run around.'

'As if I'd leave it—' But Lee was already out of the car and striding up the drive.

He had to ring the doorbell twice before it was answered. Mrs Venner opened the door just wide enough to see who he was.

Lee smiled at her. 'Good evening, Mrs Venner. If your husband at home?' And when she nodded, he said, 'I'd like a word with him, please.'

She dragged her cataracts of hair back with both hands and looked dubious.

'He's engaged at the moment. I really don't know if it would be convenient...'

'I shan't keep him long,' Lee promised, and smiled at her again. 'If you would be good enough to tell him I'm here, I'd be most grateful.'

She pulled the door wide and stood aside to let him in. 'If you'll wait here in the hall, please.' She went upstairs and disappeared beyond the half-landing. Lee heard her tap at a door, and the muted sound of voices. He thought he detected a third voice besides those of Venner and his wife.

Mrs Venner came down again. 'My husband will be with you in a moment,' she

249

said. Will you come into the lounge?'

Lee thanked her, followed her in. She indicated one of the two spindle-legged chairs which offered seating space and as he took it she plumped herself down, cross-legged, on the rug before the fire. Her fingers strayed towards a book lying there. Lee saw it was a popular romance.

'I'm sorry I have interrupted your reading,' he said pleasantly, and she shrugged but made no reply. They sat in silence for a full minute before the door was thrust open and Venner's tubby figure bounced in.

'Sergeant Lee! You must forgive me for keeping you waiting, you really must! But I was in the middle of a piece of work, and I just had to reach the end of my paragraph.' He shook his fuzzy head in what Lee took to be simulated self-reproof.

'That's all right, sir. It's me from whom an apology is due. But my visit is really necessary.'

Mrs Venner got up from the rug. 'I suppose I'd better make coffee or something, James?' She spoke vaguely.

'Not for me, thank you,' Lee said quickly. 'I'd like to get my business with Dr Venner over as soon as possible.'

'Then I'll leave you–' Mrs Venner began,

but her husband put up a hand.

'No need for you to disturb yourself, Francine, I'm sure.' He waited until she had reseated herself on the rug and picked up her book. 'Now, then Sergeant, what is it? Not that business of the youths who were hanging around here last night? I thought that was over and done with. It is as far as I'm concerned, you know.'

'They come into it, sir. As you already know, they returned after you and the constable had chased them off.'

'So I was told at your Headquarters. And I explained why they saw me go out in my car and return later, after the breakdown I had.'

Mrs Venner's eyes were on a page of her book, but Lee saw she wasn't reading it.

'They told us more than that, sir.' Lee put on a wry grin. 'The trouble is, with that type of lad it's difficult to know just when they're speaking the truth. And by the time they've told the same tale twice they start believing it themselves.'

Venner, who had seated himself in the other chair, shrugged.

'I find the same characteristic amongst my students... So what lies did these boys trot out? That's what you're leading up to, isn't

251

it? They gave you other information concerning me?'

'One of them did. You keep a ladder in your garage?'

'We do. And we lock the garage at night. We don't wish to encourage burglars.'

'This lad said they took the ladder from the garage, set it up against a window at the back. That he climbed the ladder and looked in at what seemed to be your study. That he saw you take a pistol and ammunition from beneath a loose floorboard and load the pistol.'

Mrs Venner emitted a sound which was almost a startled squeak. She covered it by a harsh clearing of her throat. Her husband gave a booming laugh.

'Judas Priest, mate, if you pigs swallow crap like that, you must have taken a real trip! Pistols, brother, are not my scene. They give me no tingle. The message has arrived, eh?'

This fellow has got knocked off balance, Lee thought. That's why he's putting on this infantile talk. He said coldly, austerely, 'You are denying the boy's statement, I take it?'

His tone seemed to sober Venner up.

'Of course I am, Sergeant! Categorically. And if it should come to a point where it is my word against that of a guttersnipe, I know which of us would be believed. No, Sergeant, the boy was completely mistaken. There is a loose floorboard in my study, and beneath it I sometimes keep a tin box with money in, when we happen to have a fairly big sum in the house. Isn't that so, Francine?'

She nodded. She was still holding her book but she was no longer interested in it. Her eyes behind her spectacles were darting speculatively between her husband's face and Lee's.

'So that point is cleared up, sir. To tell you the truth, we rather doubted the boy's story. He wasn't the leader of the gang – one of the most minor members, I'd say – and I can imagine he wanted to look big in front of the others by spinning this yarn.'

'Seen too many crook programmes on television,' Venner grunted. He was more relaxed again now. Lee was glad to see it. That was the frame of mind he wanted Venner in before he made his next move.

'There's just one other thing before I take my leave,' he said. 'We ran into your friend Edwin White today. He tried to hold up a shopkeeper near the football ground, with the object of clearing the till. Unfortunately for him he was spotted going in by a constable on duty outside the ground. He was duly arrested.'

'Hard luck on him,' Venner said casually. 'I only met him once, when Gale brought him here the other evening, as I've told you, but it struck me his IQ was far from high.' He looked at his watch and rose. 'So if that's all, Sergeant...'

Lee didn't take the hint. 'To gain favour for himself, sir, White made a serious allegation against you. He swore he saw you go into Ashcroft House last night, where Louis Pelling lived in a ground floor flat, at a time when, according to you, you were near your local post office, working on a repair to your car.'

Venner had thrust his hands into his trousers pockets. He put his head on one side and regarded Lee with a dry smile.

'A serious allegation indeed. So hadn't you better charge me with Pelling's murder straightaway? I'm going to have quite a lot of fun disproving such a charge.' He had turned to his wife, who had sprung again to her feet, staring at him. 'It's quite all right, Francine. This is really going to be a yell.'

He swung round towards Lee, his smile broadened and his eyes were almost dancing. 'Will you excuse me a moment, Sergeant, while I get the evidence?' He was shaking with internal laughter now, he seemed to be transformed in such an odd way that Lee was completely puzzled. Then Venner was out of the room, closing the door behind him. Lee heard his feet go pounding up the stairs.

Mrs Venner said abruptly, 'I'm sure there's a dreadful mistake somewhere. James wouldn't—' She broke off as she caught the sound of her husband's return down the stairs. Both she and Lee turned their eyes to the closed door, but Venner's footsteps passed it and they heard him open the front door instead. Instinctively, Lee began to get to his feet as the thought that Venner might be making some sort of breakaway hit him. Then he relaxed. If that was the idea, Dave Aston would take care of it. Indistinctly from outside he heard Venner's voice, and Mrs Venner giggled suddenly.

'It's the cat,' she said shakily. 'James is extremely fond of it and he doesn't like it staying out too long on such a damp raw night as this. He's just calling it in. Not a long business, for Marxky always comes at once.'

'Unusual name for a cat,' Lee commented.

She giggled again. 'One of James's little jokes. It's a portmanteau word, you see, made up from Marx and Trotsky. Er – do you like cats, Sergeant Lee?'

Lee said he preferred dogs, actually, but as he lived in a flat with a no-pets rule... Mrs Venner sympathized with him and for a couple of minutes they exchanged stilted conversation until Lee said, 'Your cat doesn't seem to be showing its usual obedience tonight. Dr Venner appears to be having some difficulty out there. I think I'll just–'

But he relaxed again as the front door closed with a bang. Venner came quickly into the room. He still had both hands in his trousers pockets, he still seemed to be above himself. If Lee had not known to the contrary, he would have said the chap had been on the booze.

'Sit down, Francine,' he said to his wife. 'I hate to see you just standing around.' She sank at once to the rug again and Venner turned to Lee, still laughing.

'Of course I shot Pelling,' he said. 'With this.' His right hand came out of his pocket and a Walther was thrust forward. 'You'll sit quite still, of course. It's loaded, and, having killed once, there's no reason why I shouldn't repeat what I found to be a rather enjoyable experience.'

The pistol was being held very steadily, pointing at Lee's head. The CID man had met armed killers before, he knew when they meant to carry out a threat. He said quietly, 'I don't see what good you'll do, wiping me out.'

'It might be rather pointless,' Venner agreed, 'unless you make it necessary. As it was necessary in Pelling's case. Apart from the fact that I hate his type and all it stands for, he was in my way. I need control of the underworld in this city, and he had that. Now I shall soon be in command of it.'

'And what are you going to do with it, Dr Venner?'

'I shall use it to further my aims. Oh, university students are all right when it's a mere matter of shouting and demos, but I need a body of men who, because they are against law and order, and have had experience in fighting it, will make excellent shock troops – under my leadership.' He spoke to his wife who was sitting back on her heels, staring open-mouthed at him. 'Get up, Francine. Yes, I know this is all a surprise to you, but you had it coming. On your feet, now, and find something to tie this fellow to his chair. Hurry!'

She ran, twittering foolishly, out of the room, and Lee let himself relax a little.

'I don't think you'll get away with this, you know.'

'Oh, but I shall. I'm quite prepared to make a run for it. Suitcase packed – the lot. I haven't underestimated you, Sergeant Lee. Before you get free, I'll be away I my car into that underworld I mentioned. You'll never find me.' He laughed again and with his free hand he dug into a pocket, produced two keys on a ring and flung them into one corner of the room.

'Your car keys. I guessed you wouldn't come here alone. I went down to the gate just now, told your man you wanted him to join us. I crowned him with the butt of this gun as he was getting out of the car. I don't think he's dead, but he'll be out for a while. So – nothing to stop me driving calmly away. My wife stays here, of course. I'm ditching her – and not before it's time!'

Mrs Venner had come back into the room. She was carrying a length of thin clothes line. She still seemed confused, unsure of herself.

'Tie him up, and make a good job of it. Get moving!'

'But James, I don't– I want– I mean, this is all wrong. I don't understand…'

'You don't have to. Just do as I say, or I'll shoot you both. Go on – I've no time to waste!'

Wordlessly now, Mrs Venner tied Lee's arms firmly to the chair. Under her husband's directions she cut the cord with the pocketknife he threw to her and used the rest of the line on Lee's ankles. Venner held the Walther very steadily, there was madness in his eyes but no tremor in his hand.

'Right,' he said. 'Now, you go and sit on the other chair. I shall tie you into it, now that the pig is safe.' Obediently, a woman whose brain seemed frozen with terror, she went, stiff-legged to the chair. But Venner didn't lower his gun. A crafty, calculating look had replaced the fever in his eyes.

'Come to think of it, it might be safer to shoot you both. I killed Pelling, if I'm caught I'll get what the fools call life for that. But two more deaths wouldn't make any difference, surely? Yes, it would be best to–'

An incisive voice, crisp with authority, spoke sharply from the open doorway.

'Venner! Don't be silly, boy! Drop that

thing at once!'

Venner's fingers opened, the Walther hit the rug with a thud and with a speed of movement which astonished Lee, Mrs Venner dived at it and seized it. She came upright with the pistol pointing at her husband.

'Don't give me an excuse to use it!' she gasped. I'd love to – I've wanted to for years.'

William Holder came forward and took the gun from her.

'You just set Mr Lee free,' he said soothingly. 'Then we'll sort it all out.'

Venner swung round to face him. 'Blast you, Gripper!' His voice was a sobbing scream. 'You knew damn well–'

'I didn't actually know, but I hoped the old tones would work, Venner. You've had your chips, boy. Be sensible, now.'

Lee shook off his cut ropes, took the Walther from the old schoolmaster, set the safety catch and pocketed the pistol. Venner had collapsed into the other chair, shaking.

'Good to see you, sir,' Lee said. 'How did you manage to turn up at so opportune a moment?'

'I came to see Venner this evening. I'd heard a few things about his ambitions, you see, I'd asked around amongst some of my old lads, with whom he'd tried to get in touch. We were talking in his study upstairs when you arrived, I was trying, without much success, I fear, to show him the error of his ways. He left me in the study, then later came up and locked me in there. But one of my old boys from Farley Street School once showed me how to use a wire on a lock. I found what I wanted, after some searching, in a drawer in the study. Noting how matters were here, I thought, rather desperately, that a sharp command, issued in the voice he always jumped to instinctively in former days, might throw him off balance. Happily–'

He turned his head as Aston, looking very much the worse for wear, staggered through the doorway, blinking.

'Where's that flaming Venner?' he demanded furiously. 'When I get my hands on him, I'll–'

'You'll help me to take him back to HQ, Dave,' Lee said quietly. 'Just keep an eye on him while I use the telephone.'

Chapter Seventeen

The Assistant Chief Constable's room at Benfield Police Headquarters, opulent and large, was a sanctum for a tycoon rather than for a copper. The buzz was that Grover, a junior member of one of the county families, had furnished most of that room himself, with an eventual Lord Lieutenancy in mind. He believed in the value of appearances.

Seated in a half circle before his massive, handsome desk, Superintendent Trott, Inspector Mallin and Sergeant Lee faced him, with Trott in the centre, Mallin on his right. Grover had arranged them thus. He was a firm believer in the protocol of rank. Lee, trying to fit his bulk comfortably into a chair which threatened to tip him on his back if he made an incautious move, felt some surprise that Grover hadn't ordered them to take off their shoes before entering.

But today, at any rate, Grover was showing none of the fussiness, the short temper, which his inferiors knew he could exhibit at times. He was expansive, almost beaming.

As he could well afford to be (this was Mallin's thought) when some sound, even brilliant work had been presented to him, closing a couple of cases which at one time had looked exceedingly sticky.

'I have your reports, gentlemen,' he began, and indicated a file before him. 'I have studied them with due attention and care. However, they are merely reports, setting out only the bones of your recent work, which, of course, reports should do. But now, for my personal satisfaction, you will clothe those bones with flesh for me. It is good practice for a police officer to render an oral narration, such as he will be expected to do later on in a court of law.' He looked at the small onyx and gilt clock on his desk and added, 'I can spare you half an hour if necessary. I have then to meet a deputation of senior police officers from North West Region. They are travelling across the Pennines to inspect the Mobile Murder Unit I have set up here, and which some of my own officers seem so reluctant to use.' He looked at each of them in turn but met only three pairs of black eyes. He gave a little cough. 'Will you be good enough to start off, Mr Trott?'

'I'd rather leave it to Inspector Mallin and

Sergeant Lee, sir. They did most of the field work, I acted mainly as co-ordinator.'

'As you wish. Inspector?'

Mallin paused for a moment. Then, 'Without seeming too fanciful, sir, it was a case of two lions with their attendant jackals, Pelling and Venner being the big cats. Pelling rose like a rocket almost as soon as he came to live here, we've suspected him as being behind quite a few jobs but we've never been able to pin anything on him. Thanks to Edwin White, who has talked plenty, we know Pelling had an underworld set-up which he could call upon when he needed it.'

'You'll have the names of his confederates, of course?'

'No, sir. White wouldn't grass that far. Just that there was this organization. It'll be broken up now, with Pelling's death.

'Most of the people who ran his legitimate businesses seem loyal enough, with one exception – Trent. He'd already tasted the delights of easy money in his blackmailing of Norton. He aimed to take Pelling's place eventually, though in my opinion that would have been too big a job for such a little man.

'Trent saw Venner, with his crazy ideas of revolution, and Venner himself as the

Napoleon leading his troops to anarchy, as an ideal patsy. He fed Venner's vanity from hell to breakfast, sir. Kidded him that if Pelling was wiped out, Venner could take over, using Pelling's crook organization, and the money it would bring in, for his own purposes. Venner fell for it.

'But Pelling was no fool. He realized Venner was a possible danger to such people as himself. I think Trent must have talked to Pelling about Dawson, too, possibly linking him with Venner, which is why we found the two names bracketed in Pelling's diary. This is something we have to assume, but it's partly borne out by the fact that Pelling set Jowett and his gang to keep an eye on Venner. They reported the visit of Gale and White. Trent, playing Venner along, had arranged this visit. The idea, as we gather from White, was that they, and what he calls a few more, should be the nucleus of a criminal fighting force under Venner's direction.

'Meanwhile, Wilfred Dawson had discovered that Trent was blacking Julian Norton, doing a spy act on Trent when he collected Norton's money from the Common. Dawson wanted to get hold of the photograph Mrs Norton had shown him as evidence and to use it on Norton for his own purposes. But it was locked up in Norton's house and obtaining it wasn't easy. It meant breaking into the house and searching it. Dawson saw White and Gale as the pair who would do this job – if Venner could persuade them. We know this detail from Trent's statement. Venner pretended to agree – Norton was one of the capitalist class Venner was out to destroy, and Dawson promised to share the proceeds with him. But Venner, Trent tells us, wanted to bleed Norton even harder. He told Trent he knew of the blackmailing game and said Dawson must be kept out of it. Trent claims he tried to argue Venner out of having anything to do with it, that the game had become too dangerous to go on with.

'Now we get Venner's story. He said he met Dawson in the grounds of Norton's house, on the excuse that they must case the place before setting Gale and White to do their break-in job. By arrangement between Trent and Venner, Trent was there, too. He put on a big act with the Walther he produced, threatening to shoot them both if they didn't drop the idea of interfering with his black-mailing of Norton. Venner says he pretended to agree, to back down. But Dawson was scared. He ran. He needed sanctuary and he obviously remembered that his old schoolmaster lived near.

'Some confusion arises here as to the ownership of the Walther which shot Dawson. It has never been registered, and Trent swears it belonged to Venner, who said he would use it for the purpose of scaring Dawson. Venner says he never saw it before that night, that he had no idea Trent was going to shoot Dawson when they chased him and caught up with him at Holder's back door. Venner admits he took it from Trent afterwards, and kept it – for safety, so he says.'

Mallin paused and Trott murmured, 'The little man with a big gun to back him and his damn fool ideas. That would appeal to Venner.'

Grover seemed to think it was time he picked up a few lines from the script.

'So the man Trent alleges it was Venner who took the gun and shot Dawson. Venner says Trent did it. Who can prove which of them is speaking truth?'

Lee had been rapidly turning over the pages of his notebook.

'When the Kershaws came here on Friday morning, sir, Terence Kershaw told of a snatch of conversation he heard between

Venner and Trent which seems to suggest Trent did the shooting. Venner, in effect, said he wouldn't have allowed it, if he'd had a chance to stop it. Trent told him not to worry, that everything would be all right. To which Venner replied, "Well, he's paid for it, but in future I'll give the orders, remember." It's a fair assumption that the two were then discussing the shooting of Dawson.'

Grover waved his hands. 'That's something the lawyers will have to sort out during the trial. Not our responsibility, thank God. Are there any more loose ends hanging out, or have we covered the ground?'

'I think we can depend on White's statement that saw Venner at Ashcroft House last night, sir,' Lee continued. 'I know we have Venner's confession that he killed Pelling but he might withdraw it, just to confuse the issue in Court. This has been done before. That leaves only the attack on young Kershaw in the alley to be accounted for. This was done by Jowett's gang on orders from Trent. Baker swears to this. Trent knew Kershaw had been spying on him, he had to be taught a lesson before he was dismissed from the High Swing. Trent wanted to dissuade him from talking to us.'

'There are times,' Grover said sententiously, 'when I am glad I am just the ordinary man, with the ordinary man's ambitions. Here we have Venner, in his own estimation the anarchist leader of the Seventies. And Trent, not content with a comfortable job, aching to oust Pelling from his high position. And Dawson, eager for what? To prove himself in some way?'

'Inferiority complex,' Trott supplied. 'Showed in his compulsive lying. That's always a sign.'

Grover shrugged. 'So, gentlemen, we close the file. Not much police work to show for it, really, but...'

'But,' Trott took him up, 'Pelling is dead. And that's one big headache gone. We'll have fewer big jobs pulled in this district now, and that I'll warrant.'

'Though you never could pin any evidence on Pelling, Mr Trott,' Grover reminded him tartly.

'That's also true, sir.' Trott shrugged. 'And no doubt I'll cry myself to sleep many a night, regretting it.'

The publishers hope that this book has given you enjoyable reading. Large Print Books are especially designed to be as easy to see and hold as possible. If you wish a complete list of our books please ask at your local library or write directly to:

Dales Large Print Books
Magna House, Long Preston,
Skipton, North Yorkshire.
BD23 4ND